VAMPIRES & THE SHADOW WORLD

First published in Great Britain in 2025 by Pyramid, an imprint of
Octopus Publishing Group Ltd
Carmelite House
50 Victoria Embankment
London EC4Y 0DZ
www.octopusbooks.co.uk

An Hachette UK Company
www.hachette.co.uk

The authorized representative in the EEA is Hachette Ireland,
8 Castlecourt Centre, Dublin 15, D15 XTP3, Ireland (email: info@hbgi.ie)

Distributed in the US by Hachette Book Group
1290 Avenue of the Americas, 4th and 5th Floors
New York, NY 10104

Distributed in Canada by Canadian Manda Group
664 Annette St., Toronto, Ontario, Canada M6S 2C8

ISBN 978-0-7537-3562-6

A CIP catalogue record for this book is available from the British Library.

Printed and bound in Great Britain.

10 9 8 7 6 5 4 3 2 1

Publisher: Lucy Pessell
Designer: Isobel Platt
Senior Editor: Tim Leng
Assistant Editor: Samina Rahman

Picture Credits: iStock/cozygraphic, Extezty, ggodby

VAMPIRES & THE SHADOW WORLD

AN ANTHOLOGY OF CLASSIC POETRY & STORIES

AURORA THORNE

CONTENTS

Introduction 6

VAMPIRES: TALES OF SEDUCERS & SHAPESHIFTERS

from *Dracula* • Bram Stoker 9
The Metamorphoses of the Vampire • Charles Baudelaire 15
The Vampire • Rudyard Kipling 16
from *Clarimonde* • Théophile Gautier 18
from *Christabel* • Samuel Taylor Coleridge 23
The World • Christina Rossetti 24
The Vampyre — John Stagg 25
The Giaour • George Gordon Byron 31
The Vampire • Madison Julius Cawein 32
Lamia • John Keats 33
from *Carmilla* • Joseph Sheridan Le Fanu 34
The Bride of Corinth • Johann Wolfgang von Goethe 39
The Vampire • Heinrich August Ossenfelder 40
from *Thabala the Destroyer* • Robert Southey 41
from *The Vampyre; A Tale* • John William Polidori 42
The Vampyre • James Clerk Maxwell 48
from *Lenore* • Gottfried August Bürger,
trans. Dante Gabriel Rossetti 50
from *Varney the Vampyre* • James Malcolm Rymer 53
The Vampire Bride • Henry Thomas Lidell 60
The Vampyre • John William Polidori 61
Love the Vampire • Andrew Lang 62
from *Vikram and the Vampire* • Richard F. Burton 64
The Vampyre • Charles Baudelaire 68
Oil and Blood • W B Yeats 69

GHOSTS: TALES OF SPIRITS & SHADES

from *The Flayed Hand* • Guy de Maupassant 71
Spirits of the Dead • Edgar Allan Poe 78
from *The Haunted House* •Thomas Hood 79
The Haunted Palace• Edgar Allan Poe 80
from *The Djinns* • Victor-Marie Hugo 82

The Apparition • John Donne 83
A Chilly Night • Christina Rossetti 84
Oedipus • John Dryden 86
Ghost Raddled • Robert von Ranke Graves 87
from *The Willows* • Algernon Blackwood 88
The Walker of the Snow • Charles Dawson Shanly 92
The Ghost • Charles Baudelaire 95
The Ghosts' Moonshine • Thomas Lovell Beddoes 96
The Death Coach • T Crofton Crocker 98
Ghosts • Ella Wheeler Wilcox 101
The Hour and the Ghost • Christina Rossetti 102
The Only Ghost I Ever Saw • Emily Dickinson 105
SHADOW CREATURES:
TALES OF DEATH & DARKNESS
from *The Were-Wolf* • Clemence Housman 107
Darkness and the Shadow • Edmund Clarence Stedman 113
Shadow of Nightmare • Clark Ashton Smith 114
from *The Phantom Hag* • W Bob Holland 115
The Banshee • Dora Sigerson Shorter 118
from *Macbeth* • William Shakespeare 119
from *The Witches' Sabbath* • Conrad Aiken 120
Incantation • George Parsons Lathrop 122
The Were-Wolf • Madison Julius Cawein 124
The Sick Muse • Charles Baudelaire 125
from *The Loves of the Plants* • Erasmus Darwin 126
The Dance of Death (Totentanz) • Johann Wolfgang von Goethe 127
The Banshee • Donald A Mackenzie 129
The Demon of The Gibbet • Fitz-James O'Brien 131
from *The Oni on His Travels* • William Elliot Griffis 133
from *The Devils and Evil Spirits of Babylonia* • R Campbell Thompson 137
Were-Wolf • Julian Hawthorne 138
The Hag • Robert Herrick 140
Helena • Heinrich Heine 141
Ghasta, or the Avenging Demon • Percy Bysshe Shelley 142

INTRODUCTION

Vampires and other creatures of the shadow world have served to characterize our most primal fears and desires for hundreds of years. In literature, folklore and mythology, they are often depicted as potent symbols of the forbidden, the unnatural and of course, the unknown. We are both terrified and fascinated by them in equal measure.

Vampires have captivated our imaginations for centuries. Throughout the ages, tales of blood-drinking creatures have appeared in numerous cultures, from Eastern Europe to Asia and the Pacific Rim. However, it was Gothic literature that immortalized vampires as literary icons. While John Polidori's *The Vampyre* (1819) introduced the aristocratic, mysterious vampire archetype, it was Bram Stoker's *Dracula* (1897) that made the vampire a symbol of all that the Victorians feared about sexuality, disease and the collapse of social norms. In these stories, vampires are both terrifying predators and tragic figures, embodying eternal life at the cost of their humanity.

Many other shadow creatures such as werewolves, witches, banshees, succubi and demons, though less defined but equally prevalent, explore various aspects of fear and mystery. These beings symbolize an abstract threat connected with darkness, invisibility, psychological dread and of course, death. In poetry, these beings frequently symbolize the unconscious, repressed emotions or the inevitability of death. In Edgar Allan Poe's works, for instance, shadows evoke unease and despair, such as "The Haunted Palace", where the once-glorious palace casts an ominous presence, becoming a metaphorical shadow of decay and madness.

All these preternatural creatures are often reflections of their times, adapting to societal shifts and developments. During the Romantic era, they signified fear of industrialization and separation from nature, while contemporary literature explores existential themes such as identity, isolation and immortality ethics. Yet there is always an allure and air of seduction in their presence that transcends the real and the unreal, the physical and the intangible, especially when exploring topics such as loss, transformation and love.

Ultimately, vampires and shadow creatures endure in literature and poetry because they reflect humanity. The poetry and prose collected in this book embody our fascination with mortality, our struggle with the unknown and our desire for transcendence; they stand as metaphors for the darkness within and around us, inviting us to confront our fears and embrace the complexities of our existence.

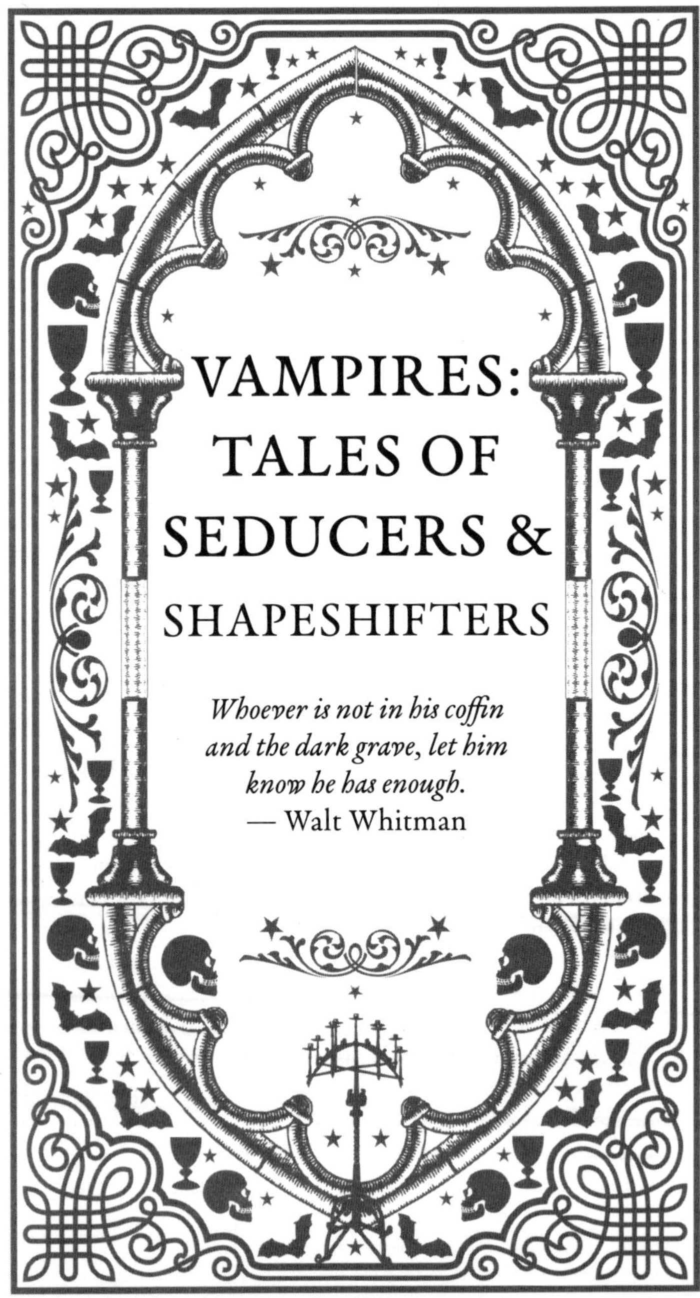

VAMPIRES: TALES OF SEDUCERS & SHAPESHIFTERS

Whoever is not in his coffin and the dark grave, let him know he has enough.
— Walt Whitman

from DRACULA

BRAM STOKER

5 May. — I must have been asleep, for certainly if I had been fully awake I must have noticed the approach of such a remarkable place. In the gloom the courtyard looked of considerable size, and as several dark ways led from it under great round arches, it perhaps seemed bigger than it really is. I have not yet been able to see it by daylight.

When the calèche stopped, the driver jumped down and held out his hand to assist me to alight. Again I could not but notice his prodigious strength. His hand actually seemed like a steel vice that could have crushed mine if he had chosen. Then he took out my traps, and placed them on the ground beside me as I stood close to a great door, old and studded with large iron nails, and set in a projecting doorway of massive stone. I could see even in the dim light that the stone was massively carved, but that the carving had been much worn by time and weather. As I stood, the driver jumped again into his seat and shook the reins; the horses started forward, and trap and all disappeared down one of the dark openings.

I stood in silence where I was, for I did not know what to do. Of bell or knocker there was no sign; through these frowning walls and dark window openings it was not likely that my voice could penetrate. The time I waited seemed endless, and I felt doubts and fears crowding upon me. What sort of place had I come to, and among what kind of people? What sort of grim adventure was it on which I had embarked? Was this a customary incident in the life of a solicitor's clerk sent out to explain the purchase of a London estate to a foreigner? Solicitor's clerk! Mina would not like that. Solicitor — — for just before leaving London I got word that my examination was successful; and I am now a full-blown solicitor! I began to rub my eyes and pinch myself to see if I were awake. It all seemed like a horrible nightmare to me, and I expected that I should suddenly awake, and find myself at home, with the dawn struggling in through the windows, as I had now and again felt in the morning after a day of overwork. But my flesh answered the pinching test, and my eyes were not to be deceived. I was indeed awake and among the Carpathians. All I could do now was to be patient, and to wait the coming of the morning.

Just as I had come to this conclusion I heard a heavy step approaching behind the great door, and saw through the chinks the gleam of a coming light. Then there was the sound of rattling chains and the clanking of massive bolts drawn back. A key was turned with the loud grating noise of long disuse, and the great door swung back.

Within, stood a tall old man, clean shaven save for a long white moustache, and clad in black from head to foot, without a single speck of colour about him anywhere. He held in his hand an antique silver lamp, in which the flame burned without chimney or globe of any kind, throwing long quivering shadows as it flickered in the draught of the open door. The old man motioned me in with his right hand with a courtly gesture, saying in excellent English, but with a strange intonation: —

"Welcome to my house! Enter freely and of your own will!" He made no motion of stepping to meet me, but stood like a statue, as though his gesture of welcome had fixed him into stone. The instant, however, that I had stepped over the threshold, he moved impulsively forward, and holding out his hand grasped mine with a strength which made me wince, an effect which was not lessened by the fact that it seemed as cold as ice — more like the hand of a dead than a living man. Again he said: —

"Welcome to my house. Come freely. Go safely; and leave something of the happiness you bring!" The strength of the handshake was so much akin to that which I had noticed in the driver, whose face I had not seen, that for a moment I doubted if it were not the same person to whom I was speaking; so to make sure, I said interrogatively: —

"Count Dracula?" He bowed in a courtly way as he replied: —

"I am Dracula; and I bid you welcome, Mr. Harker, to my house. Come in; the night air is chill, and you must need to eat and rest." As he was speaking, he put the lamp on a bracket on the wall, and stepping out, took my luggage; he had carried it in before I could forestall him. I protested but he insisted: —

"Nay, sir, you are my guest. It is late, and my people are not available. Let me see to your comfort myself." He insisted on carrying my traps along the passage, and then up a great winding stair, and along another great passage, on whose stone floor our steps rang heavily. At the end of this he threw open a heavy door, and I rejoiced to see within a well-lit room in which a table was spread for supper, and on whose mighty hearth a great fire of logs, freshly replenished, flamed and flared.

The Count halted, putting down my bags, closed the door, and crossing the room, opened another door, which led into a small octagonal room lit by a single lamp, and seemingly without a window of any sort. Passing through this, he opened another door, and motioned me to enter. It was a welcome sight; for here was a great bedroom well lighted and warmed with another log fire, — also added to but lately, for the top logs were fresh — which sent a hollow roar up the wide chimney. The Count himself left my luggage inside and withdrew, saying, before he closed the door: —

"You will need, after your journey, to refresh yourself by making your toilet. I trust you will find all you wish. When you are ready, come into the other room, where you will find your supper prepared."

The light and warmth and the Count's courteous welcome seemed to have dissipated all my doubts and fears. Having then reached my normal state, I discovered that I was half famished with hunger; so making a hasty toilet, I went into the other room.

I found supper already laid out. My host, who stood on one side of the great fireplace, leaning against the stonework, made a graceful wave of his hand to the table, and said: —

"I pray you, be seated and sup how you please. You will, I trust, excuse me that I do not join you; but I have dined already, and I do not sup."

I handed to him the sealed letter which Mr. Hawkins had entrusted to me. He opened it and read it gravely; then, with a charming smile, he handed it to me to read. One passage of it, at least, gave me a thrill of pleasure.

"I must regret that an attack of gout, from which malady I am a constant sufferer, forbids absolutely any travelling on my part for some time to come; but I am happy to say I can send a sufficient substitute, one in whom I have every possible confidence. He is a young man, full of energy and talent in his own way, and of a very faithful disposition. He is discreet and silent, and has grown into manhood in my service. He shall be ready to attend on you when you will during his stay, and shall take your instructions in all matters."

The Count himself came forward and took off the cover of a dish, and I fell to at once on an excellent roast chicken. This, with some cheese and a salad and a bottle of old Tokay, of which I had two glasses, was my supper. During the time I was eating it the Count asked me many questions as to my journey, and I told him by degrees all I had experienced.

By this time I had finished my supper, and by my host's desire had drawn up a chair by the fire and begun to smoke a cigar which he offered me, at the same time excusing himself that he did not smoke. I had now an opportunity of observing him, and found him of a very marked physiognomy.

His face was a strong — a very strong — aquiline, with high bridge of the thin nose and peculiarly arched nostrils; with lofty domed forehead, and hair growing scantily round the temples but profusely elsewhere. His eyebrows were very massive, almost meeting over the nose, and with bushy hair that seemed to curl in its own profusion. The mouth, so far as I could see it under the heavy moustache, was fixed and rather cruel-looking, with peculiarly sharp white teeth; these protruded over the lips, whose remarkable ruddiness showed astonishing vitality in a man of his years. For the rest, his ears were pale, and at the tops extremely pointed; the chin was broad and strong, and the cheeks firm though thin. The general effect was one of extraordinary pallor.

Hitherto I had noticed the backs of his hands as they lay on his knees in the firelight, and they had seemed rather white and fine; but seeing them now close to me, I could not but notice that they were rather coarse — broad, with squat fingers. Strange to say, there were hairs in the centre of the palm. The nails were long and fine, and cut to a sharp point. As the Count leaned over me and his hands touched me, I could not repress a shudder. It may have been that his breath was rank, but a horrible feeling of nausea came over me, which, do what I would, I could not conceal. The Count, evidently noticing it, drew back; and with a grim sort of smile, which showed more than he had yet done his protuberant teeth, sat himself down again on his own side of the fireplace. We were both silent for a while; and as I looked towards the window I saw the first dim streak of the coming dawn. There seemed a strange stillness over everything; but as I listened I heard as if from down below in the valley the howling of many wolves. The Count's eyes gleamed, and he said: —

"Listen to them — the children of the night. What music they make!" Seeing, I suppose, some expression in my face strange to him, he added: —

"Ah, sir, you dwellers in the city cannot enter into the feelings of the hunter." Then he rose and said: —

"But you must be tired. Your bedroom is all ready, and tomorrow you shall sleep as late as you will. I have to be away till the afternoon; so sleep well and dream well!" With a courteous bow, he opened for me himself the door to the octagonal room, and I entered my bedroom....

I am all in a sea of wonders. I doubt; I fear; I think strange things, which I dare not confess to my own soul. God keep me, if only for the sake of those dear to me!

THE METAMORPHOSES OF THE VAMPIRE

CHARLES BAUDELAIRE

Twisting and writhing like a snake on fiery sands,
Kneading her breast against her corset's metal bands,
The woman, meanwhile, from her mouth of strawberry
Let flow these fragrant words of musky mystery:
'I have the moistest lip, and well I know the skill
Within a bed's soft heart, to lose the moral will.
I dry up all your tears on my triumphant bust
And make the old ones laugh like children, in their lust.
I take the place for those who see my naked arts
Of moon and of the sun and all the other stars.
I am, my dear savant, so studied in my charms
That when I stifle men within my ardent arms
Or when I give my breast to their excited bites,
Shy or unrestrained, of passionate delight,
On all those mattresses that swoon in ecstasy
Even helpless angels damn themselves for me!'

When she had drained the marrow out of all my bones,
When I turned listlessly amid my languid moans,
To give a kiss of love, no thing was with me but
A greasy leather flask that overflowed with pus!
Frozen with terror, then, I clenched both of my eyes;
When I reopened them into the living light
I saw I was beside no vampire mannequin
That lived by having sucked the blood out of my skin,
But bits of skeleton, some rattling remains
That spoke out with the clacking of a weather vane,
Or of a hanging shop sign, on an iron spike,
Swung roughly by the wind on gusty winter nights.

THE VAMPIRE

RUDYARD KIPLING

A fool there was and he made his prayer
(Even as you and I!)
To a rag and a bone and a hank of hair
(We called her the woman who did not care),
But the fool he called her his lady fair
(Even as you and I!)

Oh the years we waste and the tears we waste
And the work of our head and hand,
Belong to the woman who did not know
(And now we know that she never could know)
And did not understand.

A fool there was and his goods he spent
(Even as you and I!)
Honor and faith and a sure intent
But a fool must follow his natural bent
(And it wasn't the least what the lady meant),
(Even as you and I!)

Oh the toil we lost and the spoil we lost
And the excellent things we planned,
Belong to the woman who didn't know why
(And now we know she never knew why)
And did not understand.

The fool we stripped to his foolish hide
(Even as you and I!)
Which she might have seen when she threw him aside,
(But it isn't on record the lady tried)
So some of him lived but the most of him died,
(Even as you and I!)

And it isn't the shame and it isn't the blame
That stings like a white hot brand.
It's coming to know that she never knew why
(Seeing at last she could never know why)
And never could understand.

from CLARIMONDE

THÉOPHILE GAUTIER

For some time the health of Clarimonde had not been so good as usual; her complexion grew paler day by day. The physicians who were summoned could not comprehend the nature of her malady and knew not how to treat it. They all prescribed some insignificant remedies, and never called a second time. Her paleness, nevertheless, visibly increased, and she became colder and colder, until she seemed almost as white and dead as upon that memorable night in the unknown castle. I grieved with anguish unspeakable to behold her thus slowly perishing; and she, touched by my agony, smiled upon me sweetly and sadly with the fateful smile of those who feel that they must die.

One morning I was seated at her bedside, and breakfasting from a little table placed close at hand, so that I might not be obliged to leave her for a single instant. In the act of cutting some fruit I accidentally inflicted rather a deep gash on my finger. The blood immediately gushed forth in a little purple jet, and a few drops spurted upon Clarimonde. Her eyes flashed, her face suddenly assumed an expression of savage and ferocious joy such as I had never before observed in her. She leaped out of her bed with animal agility – the agility, as it were, of an ape or a cat – and sprang upon my wound, which she commenced to suck with an air of unutterable pleasure. She swallowed the blood in little mouthfuls, slowly and carefully, like a connoisseur tasting a wine from Xeres or Syracuse. Gradually her eyelids half closed, and the pupils of her green eyes became oblong instead of round. From time to time she paused in order to kiss my hand, then she would recommence to press her lips to the lips of the wound in order to coax forth a few more ruddy drops. When she found that the blood would no longer come, she arose with eyes liquid and brilliant, rosier than a May dawn; her face full and fresh, her hand warm and moist – in fine, more beautiful than ever, and in the most perfect health.

'I shall not die! I shall not die!' she cried, clinging to my neck, half mad with joy. 'I can love thee yet for a long time. My life is thine, and all that is of me comes from thee. A few drops of thy rich and noble blood, more precious and more potent than all the elixirs of the earth, have given me back life.'

This scene long haunted my memory, and inspired me with strange doubts in regard to Clarimonde; and the same evening, when slumber had transported me to my presbytery, I beheld the Abbé Sérapion, graver and more anxious of aspect than ever. He gazed attentively at me, and sorrowfully exclaimed: 'Not content with losing your soul, you now desire also to lose your body. Wretched young man, into how terrible a plight have you fallen!' The tone in which he uttered these words powerfully affected me, but in spite of its vividness even that impression was soon dissipated, and a thousand other cares erased it from my mind. At last one evening, while looking into a mirror whose traitorous position she had not taken into account, I saw Clarimonde in the act of emptying a powder into the cup of spiced wine which she had long been in the habit of preparing after our repasts. I took the cup, feigned to carry it to my lips, and then placed it on the nearest article of furniture as though intending to finish it at my leisure. Taking advantage of a moment when the fair one's back was turned, I threw the contents under the table, after which I retired to my chamber and went to bed, fully resolved not to sleep, but to watch and discover what should come of all this mystery. I did not have to wait long, Clarimonde entered in her nightdress, and having removed her apparel, crept into bed and lay down beside me. When she felt assured that I was asleep, she bared my arm, and drawing a gold pin from her hair, commenced to murmur in a low voice:

'One drop, only one drop! One ruby at the end of my needle.... Since thou lovest me yet, I must not die!... Ah, poor love! His beautiful blood, so brightly purple, I must drink it. Sleep, my only treasure! Sleep, my god, my child! I will do thee no harm; I will only take of thy life what I must to keep my own from being for ever extinguished. But that I love thee so much, I could well resolve to have other lovers whose veins I could drain; but since I have known thee all other men have become hateful to me.... Ah, the beautiful arm! How round it is! How white it is! How shall I ever dare to prick this pretty blue vein!' And while thus murmuring to herself she wept, and I felt her tears raining on my arm as she clasped it with her hands. At last she took the resolve, slightly punctured me with her pin, and commenced to suck up the blood which oozed from the place. Although she swallowed only a few drops, the fear of weakening me soon seized her, and she carefully tied a little band around my arm, afterward rubbing the wound with an unguent which immediately cicatrised it. Further doubts were impossible. The Abbé Sérapion was right. Notwithstanding this positive knowledge, however, I could not cease to love Clarimonde, and I would gladly of my own accord have given her all the blood she required to sustain her factitious life. Moreover, I felt but little fear of her. The woman seemed to plead with me for the vampire, and what I had already heard and seen sufficed to reassure me completely. In those days I had plenteous veins, which would not have been so easily exhausted as at present; and I would not have thought of bargaining for my blood, drop by drop. I would rather have opened myself the veins of my arm and said to her: 'Drink, and may my love infiltrate itself throughout thy body together with my blood!' I carefully avoided ever making the least reference to the narcotic drink she had prepared for me, or to the incident of the pin, and we lived in the most perfect harmony.

Yet my priestly scruples commenced to torment me more than ever, and I was at a loss to imagine what new penance I could invent in order to mortify and subdue my flesh. Although these visions were involuntary, and though I did not actually participate in anything relating to them, I could not dare to touch the body of Christ with hands so impure and a mind defiled by such debauches whether real or imaginary. In the effort to avoid falling under the influence of these wearisome hallucinations, I strove to prevent myself from being overcome by sleep. I held my eyelids open with my fingers, and stood for hours together leaning upright against the wall, fighting sleep with all my might; but the dust of drowsiness invariably gathered upon my eyes at last, and finding all resistance useless, I would have to let my arms fall in the extremity of despairing weariness, and the current of slumber would again bear me away to the perfidious shores. Sérapion addressed me with the most vehement exhortations, severely reproaching me for my softness and want of fervour. Finally, one day when I was more wretched than usual, he said to me: 'There is but one way by which you can obtain relief from this continual torment, and though it is an extreme measure it must be made use of; violent diseases require violent remedies. I know where Clarimonde is buried. It is necessary that we shall disinter her remains, and that you shall behold in how pitiable a state the object of your love is. Then you will no longer be tempted to lose your soul for the sake of an unclean corpse devoured by worms, and ready to crumble into dust. That will assuredly restore you to yourself.' For my part, I was so tired of this double life that I at once consented, desiring to ascertain beyond a doubt whether a priest or a gentleman had been the victim of delusion. I had become fully resolved either to kill one of the two men within me for the benefit of the other, or else to kill both, for so terrible an existence could not last long and be endured. The Abbé Sérapion provided himself with a mattock, a lever, and a lantern, and at midnight we wended our way to the cemetery of — — —, the location and place of which were perfectly familiar to him. After having directed the rays of the dark lantern upon the inscriptions of several tombs, we came at last upon a great slab, half concealed by huge weeds and devoured by mosses and parasitic plants, whereupon we deciphered the opening lines of the epitaph:

Here lies Clarimonde
Who was famed in her life-time
As the fairest of women.

from
CHRISTABEL

SAMUEL TAYLOR COLERIDGE

Beneath the lamp the lady bowed,
And slowly rolled her eyes around;
Then drawing in her breath aloud,
Like one that shuddered, she unbound
The cincture from beneath her breast:
Her silken robe, and inner vest,
Dropt to her feet, and full in view,
Behold! her bosom, and half her side —
A sight to dream of, not to tell!
O shield her! shield sweet Christabel!

Yet Geraldine nor speaks nor stirs;
Ah! what a stricken look was hers!
Deep from within she seems half-way
To lift some weight with sick assay,
And eyes the maid and seeks delay;
Then suddenly as one defied
Collects herself in scorn and pride,
And lay down by the Maiden's side! —
And in her arms the maid she took,
Ah wel-a-day!
And with low voice and doleful look
These words did say:
'In the touch of this bosom there worketh a spell,
Which is lord of thy utterance, Christabel!

THE WORLD

CHRISTINA ROSSETTI

By day she wooes me, soft, exceeding fair:
But all night as the moon so changeth she;
Loathsome and foul with hideous leprosy,
And subtle serpents gliding in her hair.
By day she wooes me to the outer air,
Ripe fruits, sweet flowers, and full satiety:
But through the night, a beast she grins at me,
A very monster void of love and prayer.
By day she stands a lie: by night she stands,
In all the naked horror of the truth,
With pushing horns and clawed and clutching hands.
Is this a friend indeed; that I should sell
My soul to her, give her my life and youth,
Till my feet, cloven too, take hold on hell?

THE VAMPYRE

JOHN STAGG

"Why looks my lord so deadly pale?
Why fades the crimson from his cheek?
What can my dearest husband ail?
Thy heartfelt cares, O Herman, speak!

"Why, at the silent hour of rest,
Dost thou in sleep so sadly mourn?
Has tho' with heaviest grief oppress'd,
Griefs too distressful to be borne.

"Why heaves thy breast? — why throbs thy heart?
O speak! and if there be relief
Thy Gertrude solace shall impart,
If not, at least shall share thy grief.

"Wan is that cheek, which once the bloom
Of manly beauty sparkling shew'd;
Dim are those eyes, in pensive gloom,
That late with keenest lustre glow'd.

"Say why, too, at the midnight hour,
You sadly pant and tug for breath,
As if some supernat'ral pow'r
Were pulling you away to death?

"Restless, tho' sleeping, still you groan,
And with convulsive horror start;
O Herman! to thy wife make known
That grief which preys upon thy heart."

* * *

"O Gertrude! how shall I relate
Th' uncommon anguish that I feel;
Strange as severe is this my fate, —
A fate I cannot long conceal.

"In spite of all my wonted strength,
Stern destiny has seal'd my doom;
The dreadful malady at length
Wil drag me to the silent tomb!"

"But say, my Herman, what's the cause
Of this distress, and all thy care.
That, vulture-like, thy vitals gnaws,
And galls thy bosom with despair?

"Sure this can be no common grief,
Sure this can be no common pain?
Speak, if this world contain relief,
That soon thy Gertrude shall obtain."

"O Gertrude, 'tis a horrid cause,
O Gertrude, 'tis unusual care,
That, vulture-like, my vitals gnaws,
And galls my bosom with despair.

"Young Sigismund, my once dear friend,
But lately he resign'd his breath;
With others I did him attend
Unto the silent house of death.

"For him I wept, for him I mourn'd,
Paid all to friendship that was due;
But sadly friendship is return'd,
Thy Herman he must follow too!

"Must follow to the gloomy grave,
In spite of human art or skill;
No pow'r on earth my life can save,
'Tis fate's unalterable will!

"Young Sigismund, my once dear friend,
But now my persecutor foul,
Doth his malevolence extend
E'en to the torture of my soul.

"By night, when, wrapt in soundest sleep,
All mortals share a soft repose,
My soul doth dreadful vigils keep,
More keen than which hell scarely knows.

"From the drear mansion of the tomb,
From the low regions of the dead,
The ghost of Sigismund doth roam,
And dreadful haunts me in my bed!

"There, vested in infernal guise,
(By means to me not understood,)
Close to my side the goblin lies,
And drinks away my vital blood!

"Sucks from my veins the streaming life,
And drains the fountain of my heart!
O Gertrude, Gertrude! dearest wife!
Unutterable is my smart.

"When surfeited, the goblin dire,
With banqueting by suckled gore,
Will to his sepulchre retire,
Till night invites him forth once more.

* * *

"Then will he dreadfully return,
And from my veins life's juices drain;
Whilst, slumb'ring, I with anguish mourn,
And toss with agonizing pain!

"Already I'm exhausted, spent;
His carnival is nearly o'er,
My soul with agony is rent,
To-morrow I shall be no more!

"But, O my Gertrude! dearest wife!
The keenest pangs hath last remain'd –
When dead, I too shall seek thy life,
Thy blood by Herman shall be drain'd!

"But to avoid this horrid fate,
Soon as I'm dead and laid in earth,
Drive thro' my corpse a jav'lin straight; –
This shall prevent my coming forth.

"O watch with me, this last sad night,
Watch in your chamber here alone,
But carefully conceal the light
Until you hear my parting groan.

"Then at what time the vesper-bell
Of yonder convent shall be toll'd,
That peal shall ring my passing knell,
And Herman's body shall be cold!

"Then, and just then, thy lamp make bare,
The starting ray, the bursting light,
Shall from my side the goblin scare,
And shew him visible to sight!"

The live-long night poor Gertrude sate,
Watch'd by her sleeping, dying lord;
The live-long night she mourn'd his fate,
The object whom her soul ador'd.

Then at what time the vesper-bell
Of yonder convent sadly toll'd,
The, then was peal'd his passing knell,
The hapless Herman he was cold!

Just at that moment Gertrude drew
From 'neath her cloak the hidden light;
When, dreadful! she beheld in view
The shade of Sigismund! — sad sight!

Indignant roll'd his ireful eyes,
That gleam'd with wild horrific stare;
And fix'd a moment with surprise,
Beheld aghast th' enlight'ning glare.

His jaws cadaverous were besmear'd
With clott'd carnage o'er and o'er,
And all his horrid whole appear'd
Distent, and fill'd with human gore!

With hideous scowl the spectre fled;
She shriek'd aloud; — then swoon'd away!
The hapless Herman in his bed,
All pale, a lifeless body lay!

Next day in council 'twas decree,
(Urg'd at the instance of the state,)
That shudd'ring nature should be freed
From pests like these ere 'twas too late.

* * *

The choir then burst the fun'ral dome
Where Sigismund was lately laid,
And found him, tho' within the tomb,
Still warm as life, and undecay'd.

With blood his visage was distain'd,
Ensanguin'd were his frightful eyes,
Each sign of former life remain'd,
Save that all motionless he lies.

The corpse of Herman they contrive
To the same sepulchre to take,
And thro' both carcases they drive,
Deep in the earth, a sharpen'd stake!

By this was finish'd their career,
Thro' this no longer they can roam;
From them their friends have nought to fear,
Both quiet keep the slumb'ring tomb.

THE GIAOUR

GEORGE GORDON BYRON

... Unquenched, unquenchable,
Around, within, thy heart shall dwell;
Nor ear can hear nor tongue can tell
The tortures of that inward hell!
But first, on earth as vampire sent,
Thy corse shall from its tomb be rent:
Then ghastly haunt thy native place,
And suck the blood of all thy race;
There from thy daughter, sister, wife,
At midnight drain the stream of life;
Yet loathe the banquet which perforce
Must feed thy livid living corse:
Thy victims ere they yet expire
Shall know the demon for their sire,
As cursing thee, thou cursing them,
Thy flowers are withered on the stem.
But one that for thy crime must fall,
The youngest, most beloved of all,
Shall bless thee with a father's name —
That word shall wrap thy heart in flame!
Yet must thou end thy task, and mark
Her cheek's last tinge, her eye's last spark,
And the last glassy glance must view
Which freezes o'er its lifeless blue;
Then with unhallowed hand shalt tear
The tresses of her yellow hair,
Of which in life a lock when shorn
Affection's fondest pledge was worn,
But now is borne away by thee,
Memorial of thine agony!

THE VAMPIRE

MADISON JULIUS CAWEIN

A lily in a twilight place?
A moonflow'r in the lonely night? —
Strange beauty of a woman's face
Of wildflow'r-white!

The rain that hangs a star's green ray
Slim on a leaf-point's restlessness,
Is not so glimmering green and gray
As was her dress.

I drew her dark hair from her eyes,
And in their deeps beheld a while
Such shadowy moonlight as the skies
Of Hell may smile.

She held her mouth up redly wan,
And burning cold, - I bent and kissed
Such rosy snow as some wild dawn
Makes of a mist.

God shall not take from me that hour,
When round my neck her white arms clung!
When 'neath my lips, like some fierce flower,
Her white throat swung!

Or words she murmured while she leaned!
Witch-words, she holds me softly by, —
The spell that binds me to a fiend
Until I die.

LAMIA

JOHN KEATS

Left to herself, the serpent now began
To change; her elfin blood in madness ran,
Her mouth foam'd, and the grass, therewith besprent,
Wither'd at dew so sweet and virulent;
Her eyes in torture fix'd, and anguish drear,
Hot, glaz'd, and wide, with lid-lashes all sear,
Flash'd phosphor and sharp sparks, without one cooling tear.
The colours all inflam'd throughout her train,
She writh'd about, convuls'd with scarlet pain:
A deep volcanian yellow took the place
Of all her milder-mooned body's grace;
And, as the lava ravishes the mead,
Spoilt all her silver mail, and golden brede;
Made gloom of all her frecklings, streaks and bars,
Eclips'd her crescents, and lick'd up her stars:
So that, in moments few, she was undrest
Of all her sapphires, greens, and amethyst,
And rubious-argent: of all these bereft,
Nothing but pain and ugliness were left.

from CARMILLA

JOSEPH SHERIDAN LE FANU

In Styria, we, though by no means magnificent people, inhabit a castle, or schloss. A small income, in that part of the world, goes a great way. Eight or nine hundred a year does wonders. Scantily enough ours would have answered among wealthy people at home. My father is English, and I bear an English name, although I never saw England. But here, in this lonely and primitive place, where everything is so marvelously cheap, I really don't see how ever so much more money would at all materially add to our comforts, or even luxuries.

My father was in the Austrian service, and retired upon a pension and his patrimony, and purchased this feudal residence, and the small estate on which it stands, a bargain.

Nothing can be more picturesque or solitary. It stands on a slight eminence in a forest. The road, very old and narrow, passes in front of its drawbridge, never raised in my time, and its moat, stocked with perch, and sailed over by many swans, and floating on its surface white fleets of water lilies.

Over all this the schloss shows its many-windowed front; its towers, and its Gothic chapel.

The forest opens in an irregular and very picturesque glade before its gate, and at the right a steep Gothic bridge carries the road over a stream that winds in deep shadow through the wood. I have said that this is a very lonely place. Judge whether I say truth. Looking from the hall door towards the road, the forest in which our castle stands extends fifteen miles to the right, and twelve to the left. The nearest inhabited village is about seven of your English miles to the left. The nearest inhabited schloss of any historic associations, is that of old General Spielsdorf, nearly twenty miles away to the right.

I have said "the nearest inhabited village," because there is, only three miles westward, that is to say in the direction of General Spielsdorf's schloss, a ruined village, with its quaint little church, now roofless, in the aisle of which are the moldering tombs of the proud family of Karnstein, now extinct, who once owned the equally desolate chateau which, in the thick of the forest, overlooks the silent ruins of the town.

Respecting the cause of the desertion of this striking and melancholy spot, there is a legend which I shall relate to you another time.

I must tell you now, how very small is the party who constitute the inhabitants of our castle. I don't include servants, or those dependents who occupy rooms in the buildings attached to the schloss. Listen, and wonder! My father, who is the kindest man on earth, but growing old; and I, at the date of my story, only nineteen. Eight years have passed since then.

I and my father constituted the family at the schloss. My mother, a Styrian lady, died in my infancy, but I had a good-natured governess, who had been with me from, I might almost say, my infancy. I could not remember the time when her fat, benignant face was not a familiar picture in my memory.

This was Madame Perrodon, a native of Berne, whose care and good nature now in part supplied to me the loss of my mother, whom I do not even remember, so early I lost her. She made a third at our little dinner party. There was a fourth, Mademoiselle De Lafontaine, a lady such as you term, I believe, a "finishing governess." She spoke French and German, Madame Perrodon French and broken English, to which my father and I added English, which, partly to prevent its becoming a lost language among us, and partly from patriotic motives, we spoke every day. The consequence was a Babel, at which strangers used to laugh, and which I shall make no attempt to reproduce in this narrative. And there were two or three young lady friends besides, pretty nearly of my own age, who were occasional visitors, for longer or shorter terms; and these visits I sometimes returned.

These were our regular social resources; but of course there were chance visits from "neighbors" of only five or six leagues distance. My life was, notwithstanding, rather a solitary one, I can assure you.

My gouvernantes had just so much control over me as you might conjecture such sage persons would have in the case of a rather spoiled girl, whose only parent allowed her pretty nearly her own way in everything.

The first occurrence in my existence, which produced a terrible impression upon my mind, which, in fact, never has been effaced, was one of the very earliest incidents of my life which I can recollect. Some people will think it so trifling that it should not be recorded here. You will see, however, by-and-by, why I mention it. The nursery, as it was called, though I had it all to myself, was a large room in the upper story of the castle, with a steep oak roof. I can't have been more than six years old, when one night I awoke, and looking round the room from my bed, failed to see the nursery maid. Neither was my nurse there; and I thought myself alone. I was not frightened, for I was one of those happy children who are studiously kept in ignorance of ghost stories, of fairy tales, and of all such lore as makes us cover up our heads when the door cracks suddenly, or the flicker of an expiring candle makes the shadow of a bedpost dance upon the wall, nearer to our faces. I was vexed and insulted at finding myself, as I conceived, neglected, and I began to whimper, preparatory to a hearty bout of roaring; when to my surprise, I saw a solemn, but very pretty face looking at me from the side of the bed. It was that of a young lady who was kneeling, with her hands under the coverlet. I looked at her with a kind of pleased wonder, and ceased whimpering. She caressed me with her hands, and lay down beside me on the bed, and drew me towards her, smiling; I felt immediately delightfully soothed, and fell asleep again. I was wakened by a sensation as if two needles ran into my breast very deep at the same moment, and I cried loudly. The lady started back, with her eyes fixed on me, and then slipped down upon the floor, and, as I thought, hid herself under the bed.

I was now for the first time frightened, and I yelled with all my might and main. Nurse, nursery maid, housekeeper, all came running in, and hearing my story, they made light of it, soothing me all they could meanwhile. But, child as I was, I could perceive that their faces were pale with an unwonted look of anxiety, and I saw them look under the bed, and about the room, and peep under tables and pluck open cupboards; and the housekeeper whispered to the nurse: "Lay your hand along that hollow in the bed; someone did lie there, so sure as you did not; the place is still warm."

I remember the nursery maid petting me, and all three examining my chest, where I told them I felt the puncture, and pronouncing that there was no sign visible that any such thing had happened to me.

The housekeeper and the two other servants who were in charge of the nursery, remained sitting up all night; and from that time a servant always sat up in the nursery until I was about fourteen.

I was very nervous for a long time after this. A doctor was called in, he was pallid and elderly. How well I remember his long saturnine face, slightly pitted with smallpox, and his chestnut wig. For a good while, every second day, he came and gave me medicine, which of course I hated.

The morning after I saw this apparition I was in a state of

terror, and could not bear to be left alone, daylight though it was, for a moment.

I remember my father coming up and standing at the bedside, and talking cheerfully, and asking the nurse a number of questions, and laughing very heartily at one of the answers; and patting me on the shoulder, and kissing me, and telling me not to be frightened, that it was nothing but a dream and could not hurt me.

But I was not comforted, for I knew the visit of the strange woman was not a dream; and I was awfully frightened.

I was a little consoled by the nursery maid's assuring me that it was she who had come and looked at me, and lain down beside me in the bed, and that I must have been half-dreaming not to have known her face. But this, though supported by the nurse, did not quite satisfy me.

I remembered, in the course of that day, a venerable old man, in a black cassock, coming into the room with the nurse and housekeeper, and talking a little to them, and very kindly to me; his face was very sweet and gentle, and he told me they were going to pray, and joined my hands together, and desired me to say, softly, while they were praying, "Lord hear all good prayers for us, for Jesus' sake." I think these were the very words, for I often repeated them to myself, and my nurse used for years to make me say them in my prayers.

I remembered so well the thoughtful sweet face of that white-haired old man, in his black cassock, as he stood in that rude, lofty, brown room, with the clumsy furniture of a fashion three hundred years old about him, and the scanty light entering its shadowy atmosphere through the small lattice. He kneeled, and the three women with him, and he prayed aloud with an earnest quavering voice for, what appeared to me, a long time. I forget all my life preceding that event, and for some time after it is all obscure also, but the scenes I have just described stand out vivid as the isolated pictures of the phantasmagoria surrounded by darkness.

THE BRIDE OF CORINTH

JOHANN WOLFGANG VON GOETHE

"From my grave to wander I am forc'd
Still to seek The God's long-sever'd link,
Still to love the bridegroom I have lost,
And the life-blood of his heart to drink;
When his race is run,
I must hasten on,
And the young must 'neath my vengeance sink.

"Beauteous youth! no longer mayst thou live;
Here must shrivel up thy form so fair;
Did not I to thee a token give.
Taking in return this lock of hair?
View it to thy sorrow!
Grey thou'lt be to-morrow,
Only to grow brown again when there."

"Mother, to this final prayer give ear!
Let a funeral pile be straightway dress'd;
Open then my cell so sad and drear,
That the flames may give the lovers rest!
When ascends the fire
From the glowing pyre,
To the gods of old we'll hasten, blest."

THE VAMPIRE

HEINRICH AUGUST OSSENFELDER

My dear young maiden clingeth
Unbending fast and firm
To all the long-held teaching
Of a mother ever true;
As in vampires unmortal
Folk on the Theyse's portal
Heyduck-like do believe.
But my Christine thou dost dally,
And wilt my loving parry
Till I myself avenging
To a vampire's health a-drinking
Him toast in pale tockay.

And as softly thou art sleeping
To thee shall I come creeping
And thy life's blood drain away.
And so shalt thou be trembling
For thus shall I be kissing
And death's threshold thou' it be crossing
With fear, in my cold arms.
And last shall I thee question
Compared to such instruction
What are a mother's charms?

from THABALA THE DESTROYER

ROBERT SOUTHEY

The Cryer from the Minaret
Proclaimed the midnight hour;
"Now! now!" cried Thalaba,
And o'er the chamber of the tomb
There spread a lurid gleam
Like the reflection of a sulphur fire,
And in that hideous light
Oneiza stood before them, it was She,
Her very lineaments, and such as death
Had changed them, livid cheeks, and lips of blue.
But in her eyes there dwelt
Brightness more terrible
Than all the loathsomeness of death.
"Still art thou living, wretch?"
In hollow tones she cried to Thalaba,
"And must I nightly leave my grave
"To tell thee, still in vain,
"God has abandoned thee?"

"This is not she!" the Old Man exclaimed,
"A Fiend! a manifest Fiend!"
And to the youth he held his lance,
"Strike and deliver thyself!"
"Strike her!" cried Thalaba,
And palsied of all powers
Gazed fixedly upon the dreadful form.
"Yea! strike her!" cried a voice whose tones
Flowed with such sudden healing thro' his soul,

***

As when the desert shower. From death delivered him.
But unobedient to that well-known voice
His eye was seeking it,
When Moath firm of heart,
Performed the bidding; thro' the vampire corpse
He thrust his lance; it fell,
And howling with the wound
Its demon tenant fled.
A sapphire light fell on them,
And garmented with glory, in their sight
Oneiza's Spirit stood.

from THE VAMPYRE; A TALE

JOHN WILLIAM POLIDORI

Having left Rome, Aubrey directed his steps towards Greece, and crossing the Peninsula, soon found himself at Athens. He then fixed his residence in the house of a Greek; and soon occupied himself in tracing the faded records of ancient glory upon monuments that apparently, ashamed of chronicling the deeds of freemen only before slaves, had hidden themselves beneath the sheltering soil or many coloured lichen. Under the same roof as himself, existed a being, so beautiful and delicate, that she might have formed the model for a painter wishing to pourtray on canvass the promised hope of the faithful in Mahomet's paradise, save that her eyes spoke too much mind for any one to think she could belong to those who had no souls. As she danced upon the plain, or tripped along the mountain's side, one would have thought the gazelle a poor type of her beauties; for who would have exchanged her eye, apparently the eye of animated nature, for that sleepy luxurious look of the animal suited but to the taste of an epicure. The light step of Ianthe often accompanied Aubrey in his search after antiquities, and often would the unconscious girl, engaged in the pursuit of a Kashmere butterfly, show the whole beauty of her form, floating as it were upon the wind, to the eager gaze of him, who forgot the letters he had just decyphered upon an almost effaced tablet, in the contemplation of her sylph-like figure. Often would her tresses falling, as she flitted around, exhibit in the sun's ray such delicately brilliant and swiftly fading hues, it might well excuse the forgetfulness of the antiquary, who let escape from his mind the very object he had before thought of vital importance to the proper interpretation of a passage in Pausanias. But why attempt to describe charms which all feel, but none can appreciate? — It was innocence, youth, and beauty, unaffected by crowded drawing-rooms and stifling balls. Whilst he drew those remains of which he wished to preserve a memorial for his future hours, she would stand by, and watch the magic effects of his pencil, in tracing the scenes of her native place; she would then describe to him the circling dance upon the open plain, would paint, to him in all the glowing colours of youthful memory, the marriage pomp she remembered viewing in her infancy; and then, turning to subjects that had evidently made a greater impression upon her mind, would tell him all the supernatural tales of her nurse. Her earnestness and apparent belief of what she narrated, excited the interest even of Aubrey; and often as she told him the tale of the living vampyre, who had passed years amidst his friends, and dearest ties, forced every year, by feeding upon the life of a lovely female to prolong his existence for the ensuing months, his blood would run cold, whilst he attempted to laugh her out of such idle and horrible fantasies; but Ianthe cited to him the names of old men, who had at last detected one living among themselves, after several of their near relatives and children had been found marked with the stamp of the fiend's appetite; and when she found him so incredulous, she begged of him to believe her, for it had been remarked, that those who had dared to question their existence, always had some proof given, which obliged them, with grief and heartbreaking, to confess it was true. She detailed to him the traditional appearance of these monsters, and his horror was increased, by hearing a pretty accurate description of Lord Ruthven; he, however, still persisted in persuading her, that there could be no truth in her fears, though at the same time he wondered at the many coincidences which had all tended to excite a belief in the supernatural power of Lord Ruthven.

Aubrey began to attach himself more and more to Ianthe; her innocence, so contrasted with all the affected virtues of the women among whom he had sought for his vision of romance, won his heart; and while he ridiculed the idea of a young man of English habits, marrying an uneducated Greek girl, still he found himself more and more attached to the almost fairy form before him. He would tear himself at times from her, and, forming a plan for some antiquarian research, he would depart, determined not to return until his object was attained; but he always found it impossible to fix his attention upon the ruins around him, whilst in his mind he retained an image that seemed alone the rightful possessor of his thoughts. Ianthe was unconscious of his love, and was ever the same frank infantile being he had first known. She always seemed to part from him with reluctance; but it was because she had no longer any one with whom she could visit her favourite haunts, whilst her guardian was occupied in sketching or uncovering some fragment which had yet escaped the destructive hand of time. She had appealed to her parents on the subject of Vampyres, and they both, with several present, affirmed their existence, pale with horror at the very name. Soon after, Aubrey determined to proceed upon one of his excursions, which was to detain him for a few hours; when they heard the name of the place, they all at once begged of him not to return at night, as he must necessarily pass through a wood, where no Greek would ever remain, after the day had closed, upon any consideration. They described it as the resort of the vampyres in their nocturnal orgies, and denounced the most heavy evils as impending upon him who dared to cross their path. Aubrey made light of their representations, and tried to laugh them out of the idea; but when he saw them shudder at his daring thus to mock a superior, infernal power, the very name of which apparently made their blood freeze, he was silent.

Next morning Aubrey set off upon his excursion unattended; he was surprised to observe the melancholy face of his host, and was concerned to find that his words, mocking the belief of those horrible fiends, had inspired them with such terror. When he was about to depart, Ianthe came to the side of his horse, and earnestly begged of him to return, ere night allowed the power of these beings to be put in action; — he promised. He was, however, so occupied in his research, that he did not perceive that day-light would soon end, and that in the horizon there was one of those specks which, in the warmer climates, so rapidly gather into a tremendous mass, and pour all their rage upon the devoted country. — He at last, however, mounted his horse, determined to make up by speed for his delay: but it was too late. Twilight, in these southern climates, is almost unknown; immediately the sun sets, night begins: and ere he had advanced far, the power of the storm was above — its echoing thunders had scarcely an interval of rest — its thick heavy rain forced its way through the canopying foliage, whilst the blue forked lightning seemed to fall and radiate at his very feet. Suddenly his horse took fright, and he was carried with dreadful rapidity through the entangled forest. The animal at last, through fatigue, stopped, and he found, by the glare of lightning, that he was in the neighbourhood of a hovel that hardly lifted itself up from the masses of dead leaves and brushwood which surrounded it. Dismounting, he approached, hoping to find some one to guide him to the town, or at least trusting to obtain shelter from the pelting of the storm. As he approached, the thunders, for a moment silent, allowed him to hear the dreadful shrieks of a woman mingling with the stifled, exultant mockery of a laugh, continued in one almost unbroken sound; — he was startled: but, roused by the thunder which again rolled over his head, he, with a sudden effort, forced open the door of the hut. He found himself in utter darkness: the sound, however, guided him. He was apparently unperceived; for, though he called, still the sounds continued, and no notice was taken of him. He found himself in contact with some one, whom he immediately seized; when a voice cried, "Again baffled!" to which a loud laugh succeeded; and he felt himself grappled by one whose strength seemed superhuman: determined to sell his life as dearly as he could, he struggled; but it was in vain: he was lifted from his feet and hurled with enormous force against the ground: — his enemy threw himself upon him, and kneeling upon his breast, had placed his hands upon his throat — when the glare of many torches penetrating through the hole that gave light in the day, disturbed him; — he instantly rose, and, leaving his prey, rushed through the door, and in a moment the crashing of the branches, as he broke through the wood, was no longer heard. The storm was now still; and Aubrey, incapable of moving, was soon heard by those without. They entered; the light of their torches fell upon the mud walls, and the thatch loaded on every individual straw with heavy flakes of soot. At the desire of Aubrey they searched for her who had attracted him by her cries; he was again left in darkness; but what was his horror, when the light of the torches once more burst upon him, to perceive the airy form of his fair conductress brought in a lifeless corse. He shut his eyes, hoping that it was but a vision arising from his disturbed imagination; but he again saw the same form, when he unclosed them, stretched by his side. There was no colour upon her cheek, not even upon her lip; yet there was a stillness about her face that seemed almost as attaching as the life that once dwelt there: — upon her neck and breast was blood, and upon her throat were the marks of teeth having opened the vein: — to this the men pointed, crying, simultaneously struck with horror, "A Vampyre! a Vampyre!" A litter was quickly formed, and Aubrey was laid by the side of her who had lately been to him the object of so many bright and fairy visions, now fallen with the flower of life that had died within her. He knew not what his thoughts were — his mind was benumbed and seemed to shun reflection, and take refuge in vacancy — he held almost unconsciously in his hand a naked dagger of a particular construction, which had been found in the hut. They were soon met by different parties who had been engaged in the search of her whom a mother had missed. Their lamentable cries, as they approached the city, forewarned the parents of some dreadful catastrophe. — To describe their grief would be impossible; but when they ascertained the cause of their child's death, they looked at Aubrey, and pointed to the corse. They were inconsolable; both died broken-hearted.

Aubrey being put to bed was seized with a most violent fever, and was often delirious; in these intervals he would call upon Lord Ruthven and upon Ianthe — by some unaccountable combination he seemed to beg of his former companion to spare the being he loved. At other times he would imprecate maledictions upon his head, and curse him as her destroyer. Lord Ruthven, chanced at this time to arrive at Athens, and, from whatever motive, upon hearing of the state of Aubrey, immediately placed himself in the same house, and became his constant attendant. When the latter recovered from his delirium, he was horrified and startled at the sight of him whose image he had now combined with that of a Vampyre; but Lord Ruthven, by his kind words, implying almost repentance for the fault that had caused their separation, and still more by the attention, anxiety, and care which he showed, soon reconciled him to his presence. His lordship seemed quite changed; he no longer appeared that apathetic being who had so astonished Aubrey; but as soon as his convalescence began to be rapid, he again gradually retired into the same state of mind, and Aubrey perceived no difference from the former man, except that at times he was surprised to meet his gaze fixed intently upon him, with a smile of malicious exultation playing upon his lips: he knew not why, but this smile haunted him. During the last stage of the invalid's recovery, Lord Ruthven was apparently engaged in watching the tideless waves raised by the cooling breeze, or in marking the progress of those orbs, circling, like our world, the moveless sun; — indeed, he appeared to wish to avoid the eyes of all.

THE VAMPYRE

JAMES CLERK MAXWELL

There is a knight riding through the wood
And a doughty knight is he
And surely he delivering a message
He rides so hastily
He passes the Oak and he passes the Birch
And he passes many a tree
But pleasant to him was the tree so slim

For beneath it he did see
The bonniest lady that ever he saw
She was so shining and fair …
… But her rosy cheek grew ghostly pale
And she seemed as she was dead
And the false, false knight grew pale with fright
And his hair rose up on end.
For bygone days came to his mind
And he recognized his former love
Then the lady spoke – "Thou, false knight,
Have done me much ill
Thou didst forsake me long ago
But I am constant still.
For, though I lie in the woods so cold
I cannot be at rest
Until I suck the good life blood
Of the man who made me die."
He saw her lips were wet with blood
And he saw her lifeless eyes
And loud he cried, "Get from my side,
Thou vampire corpse unclean!"
But, no, he is in her magic boat
And on that wide, wide sea.
And the vampire sucks his good life's blood
She sucks him until he dies.
So, now, beware, whoever you are
That walks in this lone wood
Beware of that deceitful sprite
The ghost that suckles the blood.

from LENORE

GOTTFRIED AUGUST BÜRGER,

TRANS. DANTE GABRIEL ROSSETTI

"You bury your corpse at the dark midnight,
With hymns and bells and wailing; —
But I bring home my youthful wife
To a bride-feast's rich regaling.
Come, chorister, come with thy choral throng.
And solemnly sing me a marriage-song;
Come, friar, come, — let the blessing be spoken,
That the bride and the bridegroom's sweet rest be unbroken."

Died the dirge and vanished the bier: —
Obedient to his call,
Hard hard behind, with a rush like the wind,
Came the long steps' pattering fall:
And ever further! ring, ring, ring!
To and fro they sway and swing;
Snorting and snuffing they skim the ground,
And the sparks spurt up, and the stones run round.

How flew to the right, how flew to the left,
Trees, mountains in the race!
How to the left, and the right and the left,
Flew town and market-place!
"What ails my love? the moon shines bright:
Bravely the dead men ride thro' the night.
Is my love afraid of the quiet dead?"
"Ah! let them alone in their dusty bed!"

See, see, see! by the gallows-tree,
As they dance on the wheel's broad hoop,
Up and down, in the gleam of the moon
Half lost, an airy group: —
"Ho! ho! mad mob, come hither amain,
And join in the wake of my rushing train; —
Come, dance me a dance, ye dancers thin.
Ere the planks of the marriage-bed close us in."

And hush, hush, hush! the dreamy rout
Came close with a ghastly bustle,
Like the whirlwind in the hazel-bush,
When it makes the dry leaves rustle:
And faster, faster! ring, ring, ring!
To and fro they sway and swing;
Snorting and snuffing they skim the ground,
And the sparks spurt up, and the stones run round.

How flew the moon high overhead,
In the wild race madly driven!
In and out, how the stars danced about.
And reeled o'er the flashing heaven!
"What ails my love? the moon shines bright:
Bravely the dead men ride thro' the night.
Is my love afraid of the quiet dead?"
"Alas! let them sleep in their dusty bed."

"Horse, horse! meseems 'tis the cock's shrill note,
And the sand is well nigh spent;
Horse, horse, away! 'tis the break of day, —
'Tis the morning air's sweet scent.
Finished, finished is our ride:
Room, room for the bridegroom and the bride!
At last, at last, we have reached the spot,
For the speed of the dead man has slackened not!"

* * *

And swiftly up to an iron gate
With reins relaxed they went;
At the rider's touch the bolts flew back.
And the bars were broken and bent;
The doors were burst with a deafening knell,
And over the white graves they dashed pell mell:
The tombs around looked grassy and grim,
As they glimmered and glanced in the moonlight dim.

But see! but see! in an eyelid's beat,
Towhoo! a ghastly wonder!
The horseman's jerkin, piece by piece.
Dropped off like brittle tinder!
Fleshless and hairless, a naked skull,
The sight of his weird head was horrible;
The lifelike mask was there no more.
And a scythe and a sandglass the skeleton bore.

Loud snorted the horse as he plunged and reared,
And the sparks were scattered round: —
What man shall say if he vanished away.
Or sank in the gaping ground?
Groans from the earth and shrieks in the air!
Howling and wailing everywhere!
Half dead, half living, the soul of Lenore
Fought as it never had fought before.

from VARNEY THE VAMPYRE

JAMES MALCOLM RYMER

The solemn tones of an old cathedral clock have announced midnight — the air is thick and heavy — a strange, death-like stillness pervades all nature. Like the ominous calm which precedes some more than usually terrific outbreak of the elements, they seem to have paused even in their ordinary fluctuations, to gather a terrific strength for the great effort. A faint peal of thunder now comes from far off. Like a signal gun for the battle of the winds to begin, it appeared to awaken them from their lethargy, and one awful, warring hurricane swept over a whole city, producing more devastation in the four or five minutes it lasted, than would a half century of ordinary phenomena.

It was as if some giant had blown upon some toy town, and scattered many of the buildings before the hot blast of his terrific breath; for as suddenly as that blast of wind had come did it cease, and all was as still and calm as before.

Sleepers awakened, and thought that what they had heard must be the confused chimera of a dream. They trembled and turned to sleep again.

All is still — still as the very grave. Not a sound breaks the magic of repose. What is that — a strange, pattering noise, as of a million of fairy feet? It is hail — yes, a hail-storm has burst over the city. Leaves are dashed from the trees, mingled with small boughs; windows that lie most opposed to the direct fury of the pelting particles of ice are broken, and the rapt repose that before was so remarkable in its intensity, is exchanged for a noise which, in its accumulation, drowns every cry of surprise or consternation which here and there arose from persons who found their houses invaded by the storm.

Now and then, too, there would come a sudden gust of wind that in its strength, as it blew laterally, would, for a moment, hold millions of the hailstones suspended in mid air, but it was only to dash them with redoubled force in some new direction, where more mischief was to be done.

Oh, how the storm raged! Hail — rain — wind. It was, in very truth, an awful night.

There is an antique chamber in an ancient house. Curious and quaint carvings adorn the walls, and the large chimney-piece is a curiosity of itself. The ceiling is low, and a large bay window, from roof to floor, looks to the west. The window is latticed, and filled with curiously painted glass and rich stained pieces, which send in a strange, yet beautiful light, when sun or moon shines into the apartment. There is but one portrait in that room, although the walls seem panelled for the express purpose of containing a series of pictures. That portrait is of a young man, with a pale face, a stately brow, and a strange expression about the eyes, which no one cared to look on twice.

There is a stately bed in that chamber, of carved walnut-wood is it made, rich in design and elaborate in execution; one of those works of art which owe their existence to the Elizabethan era. It is hung with heavy silken and damask furnishing; nodding feathers are at its corners — covered with dust are they, and they lend a funereal aspect to the room. The floor is of polished oak.

God! how the hail dashes on the old bay window! Like an occasional discharge of mimic musketry, it comes clashing, beating, and cracking upon the small panes; but they resist it — their small size saves them; the wind, the hail, the rain, expend their fury in vain.

The bed in that old chamber is occupied. A creature formed in all fashions of loveliness lies in a half sleep upon that ancient couch — a girl young and beautiful as a spring morning. Her long hair has escaped from its confinement and streams over the blackened coverings of the bedstead; she has been restless in her sleep, for the clothing of the bed is in much confusion. One arm is over her head, the other hangs nearly off the side of the bed near to which she lies. A neck and bosom that would have formed a study for the rarest sculptor that ever Providence gave genius to, were half disclosed. She moaned slightly in her sleep, and once or twice the lips moved as if in prayer — at least one might judge so, for the name of Him who suffered for all came once faintly from them.

She has endured much fatigue, and the storm does not awaken her; but it can disturb the slumbers it does not possess the power to destroy entirely. The turmoil of the elements wakes the senses, although it cannot entirely break the repose they have lapsed into.

Oh, what a world of witchery was in that mouth, slightly parted, and exhibiting within the pearly teeth that glistened even in the faint light that came from that bay window. How sweetly the long silken eyelashes lay upon the cheek. Now she moves, and one shoulder is entirely visible — whiter, fairer than the spotless clothing of the bed on which she lies, is the smooth skin of that fair creature, just budding into womanhood, and in that transition state which presents to us all the charms of the girl — almost of the child, with the more matured beauty and gentleness of advancing years.

Was that lightning? Yes — an awful, vivid, terrifying flash — then a roaring peal of thunder, as if a thousand mountains were rolling one over the other in the blue vault of Heaven! Who sleeps now in that ancient city? Not one living soul. The dread trumpet of eternity could not more effectually have awakened any one.

The hail continues. The wind continues. The uproar of the elements seems at its height. Now she awakens — that beautiful girl on the antique bed; she opens those eyes of celestial blue, and a faint cry of alarm bursts from her lips. At least it is a cry which, amid the noise and turmoil without, sounds but faint and weak. She sits upon the bed and presses her hands upon her eyes. Heavens! what a wild torrent of wind, and rain, and hail! The thunder likewise seems intent upon awakening sufficient echoes to last until the next flash of forked lightning should again produce the wild concussion of the air. She murmurs a prayer — a prayer for those she loves best; the names of those dear to her gentle heart come from her lips; she weeps and prays; she thinks then of what devastation the storm must surely produce, and to the great God of Heaven she prays for all living things. Another flash — a wild, blue, bewildering flash of lightning streams across that bay window, for an instant bringing out every colour in it with terrible distinctness. A shriek bursts from the lips of the young girl, and then, with eyes fixed upon that window, which, in another moment, is all darkness, and with such an expression of terror upon her face as it had never before known, she trembled, and the perspiration of intense fear stood upon her brow.

"What — what was it?" she gasped; "real, or a delusion? Oh, God, what was it? A figure tall and gaunt, endeavouring from the outside to unclasp the window. I saw it. That flash of lightning revealed it to me. It stood the whole length of the window."

There was a lull of the wind. The hail was not falling so thickly — moreover, it now fell, what there was of it, straight, and yet a strange clattering sound came upon the glass of that long window. It could not be a delusion — she is awake, and she hears it. What can produce it? Another flash of lightning — another shriek — there could be now no delusion.

A tall figure is standing on the ledge immediately outside the long window. It is its finger-nails upon the glass that produces the sound so like the hail, now that the hail has ceased. Intense fear paralysed the limbs of that beautiful girl. That one shriek is all she can utter — with hands clasped, a face of marble, a heart beating so wildly in her bosom, that each moment it seems as if it would break its confines, eyes distended and fixed upon the window, she waits, froze with horror. The pattering and clattering of the nails continue. No word is spoken, and now she fancies she can trace the darker form of that figure against the window, and she can see the long arms moving to and fro, feeling for some mode of entrance. What strange light is that which now gradually creeps up into the air? red and terrible — brighter and brighter it grows. The lightning has set fire to a mill, and the reflection of the rapidly consuming building falls upon that long window. There can be no mistake. The figure is there, still feeling for an entrance, and clattering against the glass with its long nails, that appear as if the growth of many years had been untouched. She tries to scream again but a choking sensation comes over her, and she cannot. It is too dreadful — she tries to move — each limb seems weighed down by tons of lead — she can but in a hoarse faint whisper cry, —

"Help — help — help — help!"

And that one word she repeats like a person in a dream. The red glare of the fire continues. It throws up the tall gaunt figure in hideous relief against the long window. It shows, too, upon the one portrait that is in the chamber, and that portrait appears to fix its eyes upon the attempting intruder, while the flickering light from the fire makes it look fearfully lifelike. A small pane of glass is broken, and the form from without introduces a long gaunt hand, which seems utterly destitute of flesh. The fastening is removed, and one-half of the window, which opens like folding doors, is swung wide open upon its hinges.

And yet now she could not scream — she could not move. "Help! — help! — help!" was all she could say. But, oh, that look of terror that sat upon her face, it was dreadful — a look to haunt the memory for a lifetime — a look to obtrude itself upon the happiest moments, and turn them to bitterness.

The figure turns half round, and the light falls upon the face. It is perfectly white — perfectly bloodless. The eyes look like polished tin; the lips are drawn back, and the principal feature next to those dreadful eyes is the teeth — the fearful-looking teeth — projecting like those of some wild animal, hideously, glaringly white, and fang-like. It approaches the bed with a strange, gliding movement. It clashes together the long nails that literally appear to hang from the finger ends. No sound comes from its lips. Is she going mad — that young and beautiful girl exposed to so much terror? she has drawn up all her limbs; she cannot even now say help. The power of articulation is gone, but the power of movement has returned to her; she can draw herself slowly along to the other side of the bed from that towards which the hideous appearance is coming.

But her eyes are fascinated. The glance of a serpent could not have produced a greater effect upon her than did the fixed gaze of those awful, metallic-looking eyes that were bent on her face. Crouching down so that the gigantic height was lost, and the horrible, protruding, white face was the most prominent object, came on the figure. What was it? — what did it want there? — what made it look so hideous — so unlike an inhabitant of the earth, and yet to be on it?

Now she has got to the verge of the bed, and the figure pauses. It seemed as if when it paused she lost the power to proceed. The clothing of the bed was now clutched in her hands with unconscious power. She drew her breath short and thick. Her bosom heaves, and her limbs tremble, yet she cannot withdraw her eyes from that marble-looking face. He holds her with his glittering eye.

The storm has ceased — all is still. The winds are hushed; the church clock proclaims the hour of one: a hissing sound comes from the throat of the hideous being, and he raises his long, gaunt arms – the lips move. He advances. The girl places one small foot from the bed on to the floor. She is unconsciously dragging the clothing with her. The door of the room is in that direction – can she reach it? Has she power to walk? – can she withdraw her eyes from the face of the intruder, and so break the hideous charm? God of Heaven! is it real, or some dream so like reality as to nearly overturn the judgment for ever?

The figure has paused again, and half on the bed and half out of it that young girl lies trembling. Her long hair streams across the entire width of the bed. As she has slowly moved along she has left it streaming across the pillows. The pause lasted about a minute – oh, what an age of agony. That minute was, indeed, enough for madness to do its full work in.

With a sudden rush that could not be foreseen – with a strange howling cry that was enough to awaken terror in every breast, the figure seized the long tresses of her hair, and twining them round his bony hands he held her to the bed. Then she screamed – Heaven granted her then power to scream. Shriek followed shriek in rapid succession. The bed-clothes fell in a heap by the side of the bed – she was dragged by her long silken hair completely on to it again. Her beautifully rounded limbs quivered with the agony of her soul. The glassy, horrible eyes of the figure ran over that angelic form with a hideous satisfaction – horrible profanation. He drags her head to the bed's edge. He forces it back by the long hair still entwined in his grasp. With a plunge he seizes her neck in his fang-like teeth – a gush of blood, and a hideous sucking noise follows. The girl has swooned, and the vampyre is at his hideous repast!

THE VAMPIRE BRIDE

HENRY THOMAS LIDELL

"I am come — I am come! once again from the tomb,
In return for the ring which you gave;
That I am thine, and that thou art mine,
This nuptial pledge receive."

He lay like a corse 'neath the Demon's force,
And she wrapp'd him in a shroud;
And she fixed her teeth his heart beneath,
And she drank of the warm life-blood!

And ever and anon murmur'd the lips of stone,
"Soft and warm is this couch of thine,
Thou'lt to-morrow be laid on a colder bed —
Albert! that bed will be mine!"

THE VAMPYRE

JOHN WILLIAM POLIDORI

The sky is changed! – and such a change; Oh, night!
And storm and darkness, ye are wond'rous strong,
Yet lovely in your strength, as is the light
Of a dark eye in woman! Far along
From peak to peak, the rattling crags among,
Leaps the lire thunder! Not from one lone cloud,
But every mountain now hath found a tongue,
And Jura answers thro' her misty shroud,
Back to the joyous Alps who call to her aloud!

And this is in the night: – Most glorious night!
Thou wer't not sent for slumber! let me be
A sharer in thy far and fierce delight, –
A portion of the tempest and of me!
How the lit lake shines a phosphoric sea,
And the big rain comet dancing to the earth!
And now again 'tis black, – and now the glee
Of the loud hills shakes with its mountain mirth,
As if they did rejoice o'er a young; earthquake's birth,

Now where the swift Rhine cleaves his way between
Heights which appear, as lovers who have parted
In haste, whose mining depths so intervene,
That they can meet no more, tho' broken hearted;
Tho' in their souls which thus each other thwarted,
Love was the very root of the fond rage
Which blighted their life's bloom, and then departed –
Itself expired, but leaving; them an age
Of years all winter – war within themselves to wage.

LOVE THE VAMPIRE

ANDREW LANG

The level sands and grey,
Stretch leagues and leagues away,
Down to the border line of sky and foam,
A spark of sunset burns,
The grey tide-water turns,
Back, like a ghost from her forbidden home!

Here, without pyre or bier,
Light Love was buried here,
Alas, his grave was wide and deep enough,
Thrice, with averted head,
We cast dust on the dead,
And left him to his rest. An end of Love.

"No stone to roll away,
No seal of snow or clay,
Only soft dust above his wearied eyes,
But though the sudden sound
Of Doom should shake the ground,
And graves give up their ghosts, he will not rise!

So each to each we said!
Ah, but to either bed
Set far apart in lands of North and South,
Love as a Vampire came
With haggard eyes aflame,
And kissed us with the kisses of his mouth!

Thenceforth in dreams must we
Each other's shadow see
Wand'ring unsatisfied in empty lands,
Still the desirèd face
Fleets from the vain embrace,
And still the shape evades the longing hands.

from
VIKRAM AND THE VAMPIRE

RICHARD F. BURTON

At Raja Vikram's silence the Baital was greatly surprised, and he praised the royal courage and resolution to the skies. Still he did not give up the contest at once.

"Allow me, great king," pursued the Demon, in a dry tone of voice, "to wish you joy. After so many failures you have at length succeeded in repressing your loquacity. I will not stop to inquire whether it was humility and self-restraint which prevented your answering my last question, or whether it was mere ignorance and inability. Of course I suspect the latter, but to say the truth your condescension in at last taking a Vampire's advice, flatters me so much, that I will not look too narrowly into cause or motive."

Raja Vikram winced, but maintained a stubborn silence, squeezing his lips lest they should open involuntarily.

"Now, however, your majesty has mortified, we will suppose, a somewhat exacting vanity, I also will in my turn forego the pleasure which I had anticipated in seeing you a corpse and in entering your royal body for a short time, just to know how queer it must feel to be a king. And what is more, I will now perform my original promise, and you shall derive from me a benefit which none but myself can bestow. First, however, allow me to ask you, will you let me have a little more air?"

Dharma Dhwaj pulled his father's sleeve, but this time Raja Vikram required no reminder: wild horses or the executioner's saw, beginning at the shoulder, would not have drawn a word from him. Observing his obstinate silence, the Baital, with an ominous smile, continued:

"Now give ear, O warrior king, to what I am about to tell thee, and bear in mind the giant's saying, 'A man is justified in killing one who has a design to kill him.' The young merchant Mal Deo, who placed such magnificent presents at your royal feet, and Shanta-Shil the devotee-saint, who works his spells, incantations, and magical rites in a cemetery on the banks of the Godavari river, are, as thou knowest, one person — the terrible Jogi, whose wrath your father aroused in his folly, and whose revenge your blood alone can satisfy. With regard to myself, the oilman's son, the same Jogi, fearing least I might interfere with his projects of universal dominion, slew me by the power of his penance, and has kept me suspended, a trap for you, head downwards from the siras-tree.

"That Jogi it was, you now know, who sent you to fetch me back to him on your back. And when you cast me at his feet he will return thanks to you and praise your valour, perseverance and resolution to the skies. I warn you to beware. He will lead you to the shrine of Durga, and when he has finished his adoration he will say to you, 'O great king, salute my deity with the eight-limbed reverence.'"

Here the Vampire whispered for a time and in a low tone, lest some listening goblin might carry his words if spoken out loud to the ears of the devotee Shanta-Shil.

At the end of the monologue a rustling sound was heard. It proceeded from the Baital, who was disengaging himself from the dead body in the bundle, and the burden became sensibly lighter upon the monarch's back.

The departing Baital, however, did not forget to bid farewell to the warrior king and his son. He complimented the former for the last time, in his own way, upon the royal humility and the prodigious self-mortification which he had displayed — qualities, he remarked, which never failed to ensure the proprietor's success in all the worlds.

Raja Vikram stepped out joyfully, and soon reached the burning-ground. There he found the Jogi, dressed in his usual habit, a deerskin thrown over his back, and twisted reeds instead of a garment hanging round his loins. The hair had fallen from his limbs and his skin was bleached ghastly white by exposure to the elements. A fire seemed to proceed from his mouth, and the matted locks dropping from his head to the ground were changed by the rays of the sun, to the colour of gold or saffron. He had the beard of a goat and the ornaments of a king; his shoulders were high and his arms long, reaching to his knees: his nails grew to such a length as to curl round the ends of his fingers, and his feet resembled those of a tiger. He was drumming upon a skull, and incessantly exclaiming, "Ho, Kali! ho, Durga! ho, Devi!"

As before, strange beings were holding their carnival in the Jogi's presence. Monstrous Asuras, giant goblins, stood grimly gazing upon the scene with fixed eyes and motionless features. Rakshasas and messengers of Yama, fierce and hideous, assumed at pleasure the shapes of foul and ferocious beasts. Nagas and Bhutas, partly human and partly bestial, disported themselves in throngs about the upper air, and were dimly seen in the faint light of the dawn. Mighty Daityas, Bramha-daityas, and Pretas, the size of a man's thumb, or dried up like leaves, and Pisachas of terrible power guarded the place. There were enormous goats, vivified by the spirits of those who had slain Brahmans; things with the bodies of men and the faces of horses, camels, and monkeys; hideous worms containing the souls of those priests who had drunk spirituous liquors; men with one leg and one ear, and mischievous blood-sucking demons, who in life had stolen church property. There were vultures, wretches that had violated the beds of their spiritual fathers, restless ghosts that had loved low-caste women, shades for whom funeral rites had not been performed, and who could not cross the dread Vaitarani stream, and vital souls fresh from the horrors of

Tamisra, or utter darkness, and the Usipatra Vana, or the sword-leaved forest. Pale spirits, Alayas, Gumas, Baitals, and Yakshas, beings of a base and vulgar order, glided over the ground, amongst corpses and skeletons animated by female fiends, Dakinis, Yoginis, Hakinis, and Shankinis, which were dancing in frightful revelry. The air was filled with supernatural sights and sounds, cries of owls and jackals, cats and crows, dogs, asses, and vultures, high above which rose the clashing of the bones with which the Jogi sat drumming upon the skull before him, and tending a huge cauldron of oil whose smoke was of blue fire. But as he raised his long lank arm, silver-white with ashes, the demons fled, and a momentary silence succeeded to their uproar. The tigers ceased to roar and the elephants to scream; the bears raised their snouts from their foul banquets, and the wolves dropped from their jaws the remnants of human flesh. And when they disappeared, the hooting of the owl, and ghastly "ha! ha!" of the curlew, and the howling of the jackal died away in the far distance, leaving a silence still more oppressive.

THE VAMPYRE

CHARLES BAUDELAIRE

You invaded my sorrowful heart
Like the sudden stroke of a blade;
Bold as a lunatic troupe
Of demons in drunken parade,

You in my mortified soul
Made your bed and your domain;
Abhorrence, to whom I am bound
As the convict is to the chain,

As the drunkard is to the jug,
As the gambler to the game,
As to the vermin the corpse,
I damn you, out of my shame!

And I prayed to the eager sword
To win my deliverance,
And have asked the perfidious vial
To redeem my cowardice.

Alas! the vial and the sword
Disdainfully said to me;
'You are not worthy to lift
From your wretched slavery,

You fool! if from her command
Our efforts delivered you forth,
Your kisses would waken again
Your vampire lover's corpse!'

OIL AND BLOOD

W B YEATS

In tombs of gold and lapis lazuli
Bodies of holy men and women exude
Miraculous oil, odour of violet.
But under heavy loads of trampled clay
Lie bodies of the vampires full of blood;
Their shrouds are bloody and their lips are wet.

GHOSTS: TALES OF SPIRITS & SHADES

There is something haunting in the light of the moon; it has all the dispassionateness of a disembodied soul, and something of its inconceivable mystery.
— Joseph Conrad

THE FLAYED HAND

GUY DE MAUPASSANT

One evening about eight months ago I met with some college comrades at the lodgings of our friend Louis R. We drank punch and smoked, talked of literature and art, and made jokes like any other company of young men. Suddenly the door flew open, and one who had been my friend since boyhood burst in like a hurricane.

"Guess where I come from?" he cried.

"I bet on the Mabille," responded one. "No," said another, "you are too gay; you come from borrowing money, from burying a rich uncle, or from pawning your watch." "You are getting sober," cried a third, "and, as you scented the punch in Louis' room, you came up here to get drunk again."

"You are all wrong," he replied. "I come from P., in Normandy, where I have spent eight days, and whence I have brought one of my friends, a great criminal, whom I ask permission to present to you."With these words he drew from his pocket a long, black hand, from which the skin had been stripped. It had been severed at the wrist. Its dry and shriveled shape, and the narrow, yellowed nails still clinging to the fingers, made it frightful to look upon. The muscles, which showed that its first owner had been possessed of great strength, were bound in place by a strip of parchment-like skin.

"Just fancy," said my friend, "the other day they sold the effects of an old sorcerer, recently deceased, well known in all the country. Every Saturday night he used to go to witch gatherings on a broomstick; he practised the white magic and the black, gave blue milk to the cows, and made them wear tails like that of the companion of Saint Anthony. The old scoundrel always had a deep affection for this hand, which, he said, was that of a celebrated criminal, executed in 1736 for having thrown his lawful wife head first into a well — for which I do not blame him — and then hanging in the belfry the priest who had married him. After this double exploit he went away, and, during his subsequent career, which was brief but exciting, he robbed twelve travelers, smoked a score of monks in their monastery, and made a seraglio of a convent."

"But what are you going to do with this horror?" we cried.

"Eh! parbleu! I will make it the handle to my door-bell and frighten my creditors."

"My friend," said Henry Smith, a big, phlegmatic Englishman, "I believe that this hand is only a kind of Indian meat, preserved by a new process; I advise you to make bouillon of it."

"Rail not, messieurs," said, with the utmost sang froid, a medical student who was three-quarters drunk, "but if you follow my advice, Pierre, you will give this piece of human debris Christian burial, for fear lest its owner should come to demand it. Then, too, this hand has acquired some bad habits, for you know the proverb, 'Who has killed will kill.'"

"And who has drank will drink," replied the host as he poured out a big glass of punch for the student, who emptied it at a draught and slid dead drunk under the table. His sudden dropping out of the company was greeted with a burst of laughter, and Pierre, raising his glass and saluting the hand, cried:

"I drink to the next visit of thy master."

Then the conversation turned upon other subjects, and shortly afterward each returned to his lodgings.

About two o'clock the next day, as I was passing Pierre's door, I entered and found him reading and smoking.

"Well, how goes it?" said I. "Very well," he responded. "And your hand?" "My hand? Did you not see it on the bell-pull? I put it there when I returned home last night. But, apropos of this, what do you think? Some idiot, doubtless to play a stupid joke on me, came ringing at my door towards midnight. I demanded who was there, but as no one replied, I went back to bed again, and to sleep."

At this moment the door opened and the landlord, a fat and extremely impertinent person, entered without saluting us.

"Sir," said he, "I pray you to take away immediately that carrion which you have hung to your bell-pull. Unless you do this I shall be compelled to ask you to leave."

"Sir," responded Pierre, with much gravity, "you insult a hand which does not merit it. Know you that it belonged to a man of high breeding?"

The landlord turned on his heel and made his exit, without speaking. Pierre followed him, detached the hand and affixed it to the bell-cord hanging in his alcove.

"That is better," he said. "This hand, like the 'Brother, all must die,' of the Trappists, will give my thoughts a serious turn every night before I sleep."

At the end of an hour I left him and returned to my own apartment.I slept badly the following night, was nervous and agitated, and several times awoke with a start. Once I imagined, even, that a man had broken into my room, and I sprang up and searched the closets and under the bed. Towards six o'clock in the morning I was commencing to doze at last, when a loud knocking at my door made me jump from my couch. It was my friend Pierre's servant, half dressed, pale and trembling.

"Ah, sir!" cried he, sobbing, "my poor master. Someone has murdered him."

I dressed myself hastily and ran to Pierre's lodgings. The house was full of people disputing together, and everything was in a commotion. Everyone was talking at the same time, recounting and commenting on the occurrence in all sorts of ways. With great difficulty I reached the bedroom, made myself known to those guarding the door and was permitted to enter. Four agents of police were standing in the middle of the apartment, pencils in hand, examining every detail, conferring in low voices and writing from time to time in their note-books. Two doctors were in consultation by the bed on which lay the unconscious form of Pierre. He was not dead, but his face was fixed in an expression of the most awful terror. His eyes were open their widest, and the dilated pupils seemed to regard fixedly, with unspeakable horror, something unknown and frightful. His hands were clinched. I raised the quilt, which covered his body from the chin downward, and saw on his neck, deeply sunk in the flesh, the marks of fingers. Some drops of blood spotted his shirt. At that moment one thing struck me. I chanced to notice that the shriveled hand was no longer attached to the bell-cord. The doctors had doubtless removed it to avoid the comments of those entering the chamber where the wounded man lay, because the appearance of this hand was indeed frightful. I did not inquire what had become of it.

I now clip from a newspaper of the next day the story of the crime with all the details that the police were able to procure: "A frightful attempt was made yesterday on the life of young M. Pierre B., student, who belongs to one of the best families in Normandy. He returned home about ten o'clock in the evening, and excused his valet, Bouvin, from further attendance upon him, saying that he felt fatigued and was going to bed. Towards midnight Bouvin was suddenly awakened by the furious ringing of his master's bell. He was afraid, and lighted a lamp and waited. The bell was silent about a minute, then rang again with such vehemence that the domestic, mad with fright, flew from his room to awaken the concierge, who ran to summon the police, and, at the end of about fifteen minutes, two policemen forced open the door. A horrible sight met their eyes. The furniture was overturned, giving evidence of a fearful struggle between the victim and his assailant. In the middle of the room, upon his back, his body rigid, with livid face and frightfully dilated eyes, lay, motionless, young Pierre B., bearing upon his neck the deep imprints of five fingers. Dr. Bourdean was called immediately, and his report says that the aggressor must have been possessed of prodigious strength and have had an extraordinarily thin and sinewy hand, because the fingers left in the flesh of the victim five holes like those from a pistol ball, and had penetrated until they almost met. There is no clue to the motive of the crime or to its perpetrator. The police are making a thorough investigation."

The following appeared in the same newspaper next day:

"M. Pierre B., the victim of the frightful assault of which we published an account yesterday, has regained consciousness after two hours of the most assiduous care by Dr. Bourdean. His life is not in danger, but it is strongly feared that he has lost his reason. No trace has been found of his assailant."

My poor friend was indeed insane. For seven months I visited him daily at the hospital where we had placed him, but he did not recover the light of reason. In his delirium strange words escaped him, and, like all madmen, he had one fixed idea: he believed himself continually pursued by a specter.

One day they came for me in haste, saying he was worse, and when I arrived I found him dying. For two hours he remained very calm, then, suddenly, rising from his bed in spite of our efforts, he cried, waving his arms as if a prey to the most awful terror: "Take it away! Take it away! It strangles me! Help! Help!" Twice he made the circuit of the room, uttering horrible screams, then fell face downward, dead.

As he was an orphan I was charged to take his body to the little village of P., in Normandy, where his parents were buried. It was the place from which he had arrived the evening he found us drinking punch in Louis R.'s room, when he had presented to us the flayed hand. His body was inclosed in a leaden coffin, and four days afterwards I walked sadly beside the old cure, who had given him his first lessons, to the little cemetery where they dug his grave. It was a beautiful day, and sunshine from a cloudless sky flooded the earth. Birds sang from the blackberry bushes where many a time when we were children we had stolen to eat the fruit. Again I saw Pierre and myself creeping along behind the hedge and slipping through the gap that we knew so well, down at the end of the little plot where they bury the poor. Again we would return to the house with cheeks and lips black with the juice of the berries we had eaten. I looked at the bushes; they were covered with fruit; mechanically I picked some and bore it to my mouth. The curé had opened his breviary, and was muttering his prayers in a low voice. I heard at the end of the walk the spades of the grave-diggers who were opening the tomb. Suddenly they called out, the curé closed his book, and we went to see what they wished of us. They had found a coffin; in digging a stroke of the pickaxe had started the cover, and we perceived within a skeleton of unusual stature, lying on its back, its hollow eyes seeming yet to menace and defy us. I was troubled, I know not why, and almost afraid.

"Hold!" cried one of the men, "look there! One of the rascal's hands has been severed at the wrist. Ah, here it is!"

and he picked up from beside the body a huge withered hand, and held it out to us.

"See," cried the other, laughing, "see how he glares at you, as if he would spring at your throat to make you give him back his hand."

"Go," said the curé, "leave the dead in peace, and close the coffin. We will make poor Pierre's grave elsewhere."

The next day all was finished, and I returned to Paris, after having left fifty francs with the old curé for masses to be said for the repose of the soul of him whose sepulchre we had troubled.

SPIRITS OF THE DEAD

EDGAR ALLAN POE

Thy soul shall find itself alone
'Mid dark thoughts of the gray tombstone
Not one, of all the crowd, to pry
Into thine hour of secrecy.
Be silent in that solitude
Which is not loneliness for then
The spirits of the dead who stood
In life before thee are again
In death around thee and their will
Shall overshadow thee: be still.
The night tho' clear shall frown
And the stars shall not look down
From their high thrones in the Heaven,
With light like Hope to mortals given
But their red orbs, without beam,
To thy weariness shall seem
As a burning and a fever
Which would cling to thee forever.
Now are thoughts thou shalt not banish
Now are visions ne'er to vanish
From thy spirit shall they pass
No more like dew-drops from the grass.
The breeze the breath of God is still
And the mist upon the hill
Shadowy shadowy yet unbroken,
Is a symbol and a token
How it hangs upon the trees,
A mystery of mysteries!

from
THE HAUNTED HOUSE

THOMAS HOOD

O'er all there hung the shadow of a fear,
A sense of mystery the spirit daunted,
And said, as plain as whisper in the ear,
The place is haunted.

Howbeit, the door I pushed — or so I dreamed —
Which slowly, slowly gaped, the hinges creaking
With such a rusty eloquence, it seemed
That Time himself was speaking.

But Time was dumb within that mansion old,
Or left his tale to the heraldic banners
That hung from the corroded walls, and told
Of former men and manners.

Those tattered flags, that with the opened door,
Seemed the old wave of battle to remember,
While fallen fragments danced upon the floor
Like dead leaves in December.

The startled bats flew out, bird after bird,
The screech-owl overhead began to flutter,
And seemed to mock the cry that she had heard
Some dying victim utter!

A shriek that echoed from the joisted roof,
And up the stair, and further still and further,
Till in some ringing chamber far aloof
In ceased its tale of murther!

THE HAUNTED PALACE

EDGAR ALLAN POE

In the greenest of our valleys
By good angels tenanted,
Once a fair and stately palace —
Radiant palace — reared its head.
In the monarch Thought's dominion —
It stood there!
Never seraph spread a pinion
Over fabric half so fair!

Banners yellow, glorious, golden,
On its roof did float and flow,
(This — all this — was in the olden
Time long ago,)
And every gentle air that dallied,
In that sweet day,
Along the ramparts plumed and pallid,
A wingèd odour went away.

Wanderers in that happy valley,
Through two luminous windows, saw
Spirits moving musically,
To a lute's well-tuned law,
Round about a throne where, sitting
(Porphyrogene!)
In state his glory well befitting,
The ruler of the realm was seen.

And all with pearl and ruby glowing
Was the fair palace door,
Through which came flowing, flowing, flowing,
And sparkling evermore,
A troop of Echoes, whose sweet duty
Was but to sing,
In voices of surpassing beauty,
The wit and wisdom of their king.

But evil things, in robes of sorrow,
Assailed the monarch's high estate.
(Ah, let us mourn! — for never morrow
Shall dawn upon him desolate!)
And round about his home the glory
That blushed and bloomed,
Is but a dim-remembered story
Of the old time entombed.

And travellers, now, within that valley,
Through the red-litten windows see
Vast forms, that move fantastically
To a discordant melody,
While, like a ghastly rapid river,
Through the pale door
A hideous throng rush out for ever
And laugh — but smile no more.

from
THE DJINNS

VICTOR-MARIE HUGO

'Tis the Djinns' wild streaming swarm
Whistling in their tempest flight;
Snap the tall yews 'neath the storm,
Like a pine flame crackling bright.
Swift though heavy, lo! their crowd
Through the heavens rushing loud
Like a livid thunder-cloud
With its bolt of fiery might!

Ho! they are on us, close without!
Shut tight the shelter where we lie!
With hideous din the monster rout,
Dragon and vampire, fill the sky!
The loosened rafter overhead
Trembles and bends like quivering reed;
Shakes the old door with shuddering dread,
As from its rusty hinge 'twould fly!
Wild cries of hell! voices that howl and shriek!
The horrid troop before the tempest tossed -
O Heaven! — descends my lowly roof to seek:

Bends the strong wall beneath the furious host.
Totters the house as though, like dry leaf shorn
From autumn bough and on the mad blast borne,
Up from its deep foundations it were torn
To join the stormy whirl. Ah! all is lost!

THE APPARITION

JOHN DONNE

When by thy scorn, O murd'ress, I am dead
And that thou think'st thee free
From all solicitation from me,
Then shall my ghost come to thy bed,
And thee, feign'd vestal, in worse arms shall see;
Then thy sick taper will begin to wink,
And he, whose thou art then, being tir'd before,
Will, if thou stir, or pinch to wake him, think
Thou call'st for more,
And in false sleep will from thee shrink;
And then, poor aspen wretch, neglected thou
Bath'd in a cold quicksilver sweat wilt lie
A verier ghost than I.
What I will say, I will not tell thee now,
Lest that preserve thee; and since my love is spent,
I'had rather thou shouldst painfully repent,
Than by my threat'nings rest still innocent.

A CHILLY NIGHT

CHRISTINA ROSSETTI

I rose at the dead of night
And went to the lattice alone
To look for my Mother's ghost
Where the ghostly moonlight shone.

My friends had failed one by one,
Middleaged, young, and old,
Till the ghosts were warmer to me
Than my friends that had grown cold.

I looked and I saw the ghosts
Dotting plain and mound:
They stood in the blank moonlight
But no shadow lay on the ground;
They spoke without a voice
And they leapt without a sound.

I called: 'O my Mother dear, ' —
I sobbed: 'O my Mother kind,
Make a lonely bed for me
And shelter it from the wind:

'Tell the others not to come
To see me night or day;
But I need not tell my friends
To be sure to keep away. '

My Mother raised her eyes,
They were blank and could not see;
Yet they held me with their stare
While they seemed to look at me.

She opened her mouth and spoke,
I could not hear a word
While my flesh crept on my bones
And every hair was stirred.

She knew that I could not hear
The message that she told
Whether I had long to wait
Or soon should sleep in the mould:
I saw her toss her shadowless hair
And wring her hands in the cold.

I strained to catch her words
And she strained to make me hear,
But never a sound of words
Fell on my straining ear.

From midnight to the cockcrow
I kept my watch in pain
While the subtle ghosts grew subtler
In the sad night on the wane.

From midnight to the cockcrow
I watched till all were gone,
Some to sleep in the shifting sea
And some under turf and stone:
Living had failed and dead had failed
And I was indeed alone.

OEDIPUS

JOHN DRYDEN

The thought of death to one near death is dreadful!
O 'tis a fearful thing to be no more;
Or, if to be, to wander after death;
To walk as spirits do, in brakes all day;
And when the darkness comes, to glide in paths
That lead to graves; and in the silent vault,
Where lies your own pale shroud, to hover o'er it,
Striving to enter your forbidden corps,
And often, often, vainly breathe your ghost
Into your lifeless lips;
Then, like a lone benighted traveller,
Shut out from lodging, shall your groans be answered
By whistling winds, whose every blast will shake
Your tender form to atoms.

GHOST RADDLED

ROBERT VON RANKE GRAVES

"Come, surly fellow, come! A song!"
What, madmen? Sing to you?
Choose from the clouded tales of wrong
And terror I bring to you.

Of a night so torn with cries,
Honest men sleeping
Start awake with glaring eyes,
Bone-chilled, flesh creeping.

Of spirits in the web hung room
Up above the stable,
Groans, knockings in the gloom,
The dancing table.

Of demons in the dry well
That cheep and mutter,
Clanging of an unseen bell,
Blood choking the gutter.

Of lust frightful, past belief,
Lurking unforgotten,
Unrestrainable endless grief
From breasts long rotten.

A song? What laughter or what song
Can this house remember?
Do flowers and butterflies belong
To a blind December?

from THE WILLOWS

ALGERNON BLACKWOOD

Suddenly I found myself lying awake, peering from my sandy mattress through the door of the tent. I looked at my watch pinned against the canvas, and saw by the bright moonlight that it was past twelve o'clock — the threshold of a new day — and I had therefore slept a couple of hours. The Swede was asleep still beside me; the wind howled as before; something plucked at my heart and made me feel afraid. There was a sense of disturbance in my immediate neighborhood.

I sat up quickly and looked out. The trees were swaying violently to and fro as the gusts smote them, but our little bit of green canvas lay snugly safe in the hollow, for the wind passed over it without meeting enough resistance to make it vicious. The feeling of disquietude did not pass however, and I crawled quietly out of the tent to see if our belongings were safe. I moved carefully so as not to waken my companion. A curious excitement was on me.

I was halfway out, kneeling on all fours, when my eye first took in that the tops of the bushes opposite, with their moving tracery of leaves, made shapes against the sky. I sat back on my haunches and stared. It was incredible, surely, but there, opposite and slightly above me, were shapes of some indeterminate sort among the willows, and as the branches swayed in the wind they seemed to group themselves about these shapes, forming a series of monstrous outlines that shifted rapidly beneath the moon. Close, about fifty feet in front of me, I saw these things.

My first instinct was to waken my companion that he too might see them, but something made me hesitate — the sudden realization, probably, that I should not welcome corroboration; and meanwhile I crouched there staring in amazement with smarting eyes. I was wide awake. I remember saying to myself that I was not dreaming.

They first became properly visible, these huge figures, just within the tops of the bushes — immense bronze-colored, moving, and wholly independent of the swaying of the branches. I saw them plainly and noted, now I came to examine them more calmly, that they were very much larger than human, and indeed that something in their appearance proclaimed them to be not human at all. Certainly they were not merely the moving tracery of the branches against the moonlight. They shifted independently. They rose upwards in a continuous stream from earth to sky, vanishing utterly as soon as they reached the dark of the sky. They were interlaced one with another, making a great column, and I saw their limbs and huge bodies melting in and out of each other, forming this serpentine line that bent and swayed and twisted spirally with the contortions of the wind-tossed trees. They were nude, fluid shapes, passing up the bushes, within the leaves almost — rising up in a living column into the heavens. Their faces I never could see. Unceasingly they poured upwards, swaying in great bending curves, with a hue of dull bronze upon their skins.

I stared, trying to force every atom of vision from my eyes. For a long time I thought they must every moment disappear and resolve themselves into the movements of the branches and prove to be an optical illusion. I searched everywhere for a proof of reality, when all the while I understood quite well that the standard of reality had changed. For the longer I looked the more certain I became that these figures were real and living, though perhaps not according to the standards that the camera and the biologist would insist upon.

Far from feeling fear, I was possessed with a sense of awe and wonder such as I have never known. I seemed to be gazing at the personified elemental forces of this haunted and primeval region. Our intrusion had stirred the powers of the place into activity. It was we who were the cause of the disturbance, and my brain filled to bursting with stories and legends of the spirits and deities of places that have been acknowledged and worshiped by men in all ages of the world's history. But, before I could arrive at any possible explanation, something impelled me to go farther out, and I crept forward on to the sand and stood upright. I felt the ground still warm under my bare feet; the wind tore at my hair and face; and the sound of the river burst upon my ears with a sudden roar. These things, I knew, were real, and proved that my senses were acting normally. Yet the figures still rose from earth to heaven, silent, majestically, in a great spiral of grace and strength that overwhelmed me at length with a genuine deep emotion of worship. I felt that I must fall down and worship — absolutely worship.

Perhaps in another minute I might have done so, when a gust of wind swept against me with such force that it blew me sideways, and I nearly stumbled and fell. It seemed to shake the dream violently out of me. At least it gave me another point of view somehow. The figures still remained, still ascended into heaven from the heart of the night, but my reason at last began to assert itself. It must be a subjective experience, I argued — none the less real for that, but still subjective. The moonlight and the branches combined to work out these pictures upon the mirror of my imagination, and for some reason I projected them outwards and made them appear objective. I knew this must be the case, of course. I was the subject of a vivid and interesting hallucination. I took courage, and began to move forward across the open patches of sand. By Jove, though, was it all hallucination? Was it merely subjective? Did not my reason argue in the old futile way from the little standard of the known?

I only know that great column of figures ascended darkly into the sky for what seemed a very long period of time, and with a very complete measure of reality as most men are accustomed to gauge reality. Then suddenly they were gone! And, once they were gone and the immediate wonder of their great presence had passed, fear came down upon me with a cold rush. The esoteric meaning of this lonely and haunted region suddenly flamed up within me and I began to tremble dreadfully. I took a quick look round — a look of horror that came near to panic — calculating vainly ways of escape; and then, realizing how helpless I was to achieve anything really effective, I crept back silently into the tent and lay down again upon my sandy mattress, first lowering the door-curtain to shut out the sight of the willows in the moonlight, and then burying my head as deeply as possible beneath the blankets to deaden the sound of the terrifying wind.

THE WALKER OF THE SNOW

CHARLES DAWSON SHANLY

Speed on, speed on, good master!
The camp lies far away;
We must cross the haunted valley
Before the close of day.

How the snow-blight came upon me
I will tell you as we go, —
The blight of the Shadow-hunter,
Who walks the midnight snow.

To the cold December heaven
Came the pale moon and the stars,
As the yellow sun was sinking
Behind the purple bars.

The snow was deeply drifted
Upon the ridges drear,
That lay for miles around me
And the camp for which we steer.

'T was silent on the hillside,
And by the solemn wood
No sound of life or motion
To break the solitude,

Save the wailing of the moose-bird
With a plaintive note and low,
And the skating of the red leaf
Upon the frozen snow.

And said I, — "Though dark is falling,
And far the camp must be,
Yet my heart it would be lightsome,
If I had but company."

And then I sang and shouted,
Keeping measure, as I sped,
To the harp-twang of the snow-shoe
As it sprang beneath my tread;

Nor far into the valley
Had I dipped upon my way,
When a dusky figure joined me,
In a capuchon of gray,

Bending upon the snow-shoes,
With a long and limber stride;
And I hailed the dusky stranger,
As we travelled side by side.

But no token of communion;
Gave he by word or look,
And the fear-chill fell upon me
At the crossing of the brook.

* * *

For I saw by the sickly moonlight,
As I followed, bending low,
That the walking of the stranger
Left no footmarks on the snow.

Then the fear-chill gathered o'er me,
Like a shroud around me cast,
As I sank upon the snow-drift
Where the Shadow-hunter passed.

And the otter-trappers found me,
Before the break of day,
With my dark hair blanched and whitened
As the snow in which I lay.

But they spoke not as they raised me;
For they knew that in the night
I had seen the Shadow-hunter,
And had withered in his blight.

Sancta Maria speed us!
The sun is falling low, —
Before us lies the valley
Of the Walker of the Snow!

THE GHOST

CHARLES BAUDELAIRE

Softly as brown-eyed Angels rove
I will return to thy alcove,
And glide upon the night to thee,
Treading the shadows silently.

And I will give to thee, my own,
Kisses as icy as the moon,
And the caresses of a snake
Cold gliding in the thorny brake.

And when returns the livid morn
Thou shalt find all my place forlorn
And chilly, till the falling night.

Others would rule by tenderness
Over thy life and youthfulness,
But I would conquer thee by fright!

THE GHOSTS' MOONSHINE

THOMAS LOVELL BEDDOES

It is midnight, my wedded;
Let us lie under
The tempest bright undreaded,
In the warm thunder:
(Tremble and weep not! What can you fear?)
My hearts best wish is thine, --
That thou wert white, and bedded
On the softest bier,
In the ghosts moonshine.
Is that the wind? No, no;
Only two devils, that blow
Through the murderers ribs to and fro,
In the ghosts moonshine.

Who is there, she said afraid, yet
Stirring and awaking
The poor old dead? His spade, it
Is only making, —
(Tremble and weep not! What do you crave?)
Where yonder grasses twine,
A pleasant bed, my maid, that
Children call a grave,
In the cold moonshine.
Is that the wind? No, no;
Only two devils, that blow
Through the murderers ribs to and fro,
In the ghosts moonshine.

What dost thou strain above her
Lovely throat's whiteness?
A silken chain, to cover
Her bosoms brightness?
(Tremble and weep not: what dost thou fear?)
— My blood is spilt like wine,
Thou hast strangled and slain me, lover,
Thou hast stabbed me dear,
In the ghosts moonshine.
Is that the wind? No, no;
Only her goblin doth blow
Through the murderers ribs to and fro,
In its own moonshine.

THE DEATH COACH

T CROFTON CROCKER

'Tis midnight! — how gloomy and dark!
By Jupiter there's not a star! —
'Tis fearful! — 'tis awful! — and hark!
What sound is that comes from afar?

Still rolling and rumbling, that sound
Makes nearer and nearer approach;
Do I tremble, or is it the ground? —
Lord save us! — what is it? — a coach! —

A coach! — but that coach has no head;
And the horses are headless as it:
Of the driver the same may be said,
And the passengers inside who sit.

See the wheels! how they fly o'er the stones!
And whirl, as the whip it goes crack:
Their spokes are of dead men's thigh bones,
And the pole is the spine of the back!

The hammer-cloth, shabby display,
Is a pall rather mildew'd by damps;
And to light this strange coach on its way,
Two hollow skulls hang up for lamps!

From the gloom of Rathcooney churchyard,
They dash down the hill of Glanmire;
Pass Lota in gallop as hard
As if horses were never to tire!

With people thus headless 'tis fun
To drive in such furious career;
Since headlong their horses can't run,
Nor coachman be heady from beer.

Very steep is the Tivoli lane,
But up-hill to them is as down;
Nor the charms of Woodhill can detain
These Dullahans rushing to town.

Could they feel as I've felt — in a song —
A spell that forbade them depart;
They'd a lingering visit prolong,
And after their head lose their heart!

No matter! — 'tis past twelve o'clock;
Through the streets they sweep on like the wind,
And, taking the road to Blackrock,
Cork city is soon left behind.

Should they hurry thus reckless along,
To supper instead of to bed,
The landlord will surely be wrong,
If he charge it at so much a head!

Yet mine host may suppose them too poor
To bring to his wealth an increase;
As till now, all who drove to his door,
Possess'd at least one crown a-piece.

***

Up the Deadwoman's hill they are roll'd;
Boreenmannah is quite out of sight;
Ballintemple they reach, and behold!
At its churchyard they stop and alight.

"Who's there?" said a voice from the ground,
"We've no room, for the place is quite full."
"O! room must be speedily found,
For we come from the parish of Skull.

"Though Murphys and Crowleys appear
On headstones of deep-letter'd pride;
Though Scannels and Murleys lie here,
Fitzgeralds and Toonies beside;

"Yet here for the night we lie down,
To-morrow we speed on the gale;
For having no heads of our own,
We seek the Old Head of Kinsale."

GHOSTS

ELLA WHEELER WILCOX

There are ghosts in the room.
As I sit here alone, from the dark corners there
They come out of the gloom,
And they stand at my side and they lean on my chair.

There's the ghost of a Hope
That lighted my days with a fanciful glow.
In her hand is the rope
That strangled her life out.Hope was slain long ago.

But her ghost comes to-night,
With its skeleton face and expressionless eyes,
And it stands in the light,
And mocks me, and jeers me with sobs and with sighs.

There's the ghost of a Joy,
A frail, fragile thing, and I prized it too much,
And the hands that destroy
Clasped it close, and it died at the withering touch.

There's the ghost of a Love,
Born with joy, reared with hope, died in pain and unrest,
But he towers above
All the others — this ghost: yet a ghost at the best.

I am weary, and fain
Would forget all these dead: but the gibbering host
Make my struggle in vain,
In each shadowy corner there lurketh a ghost.

THE HOUR AND THE GHOST

CHRISTINA ROSSETTI

O love, love, hold me fast,
He draws me away from thee;
I cannot stem the blast,
Nor the cold strong sea:
Far away a light shines
Beyond the hills and pines;
It is lit for me.

Bridegroom
I have thee close, my dear,
No terror can come near;
Only far off the northern light shines clear.

Ghost
Come with me, fair and false,
To our home, come home.
It is my voice that calls:
Once thou wast not afraid
When I woo'd, and said,
'Come, our nest is newly made' —
Now cross the tossing foam.

Bride
Hold me one moment longer!
He taunts me with the past,
His clutch is waxing stronger;
Hold me fast, hold me fast.

He draws me from thy heart,
And I cannot withhold:
He bids my spirit depart
With him into the cold: —
Oh bitter vows of old!

Bridegroom
Lean on me, hide thine eyes:
Only ourselves, earth and skies,
Are present here: be wise.

Ghost
Lean on me, come away,
I will guide and steady:
Come, for I will not stay:
Come, for house and bed are ready.
Ah sure bed and house,
For better and worse, for life and death,
Goal won with shortened breath!
Come, crown our vows.

Bride
One moment, one more word,
While my heart beats still,
While my breath is stirred
By my fainting will.
O friend, forsake me not,
Forget not as I forgot:
But keep thy heart for me,
Keep thy faith true and bright;
Through the lone cold winter night
Perhaps I may come to thee.

* * *

Bridegroom
Nay peace, my darling, peace:
Let these dreams and terrors cease:
Who spoke of death or change or aught but ease?

Ghost
O fair frail sin,
O poor harvest gathered in!
Thou shalt visit him again
To watch his heart grow cold:
To know the gnawing pain
I knew of old;
To see one much more fair
Fill up the vacant chair,
Fill his heart, his children bear;
While thou and I together,
In the outcast weather,
Toss and howl and spin.

THE ONLY GHOST I EVER SAW

EMILY DICKINSON

The only ghost I ever saw
Was dressed in mechlin, so;
He wore no sandal on his foot,
And stepped like flakes of snow.
His gait was soundless, like the bird,
But rapid, like the roe;
His fashions quaint, mosaic,
Or, haply, mistletoe.

His conversation seldom,
His laughter like the breeze
That dies away in dimples
Among the pensive trees.
Our interview was transient,
Of me, himself was shy;
And God forbid I look behind
Since that appalling day!

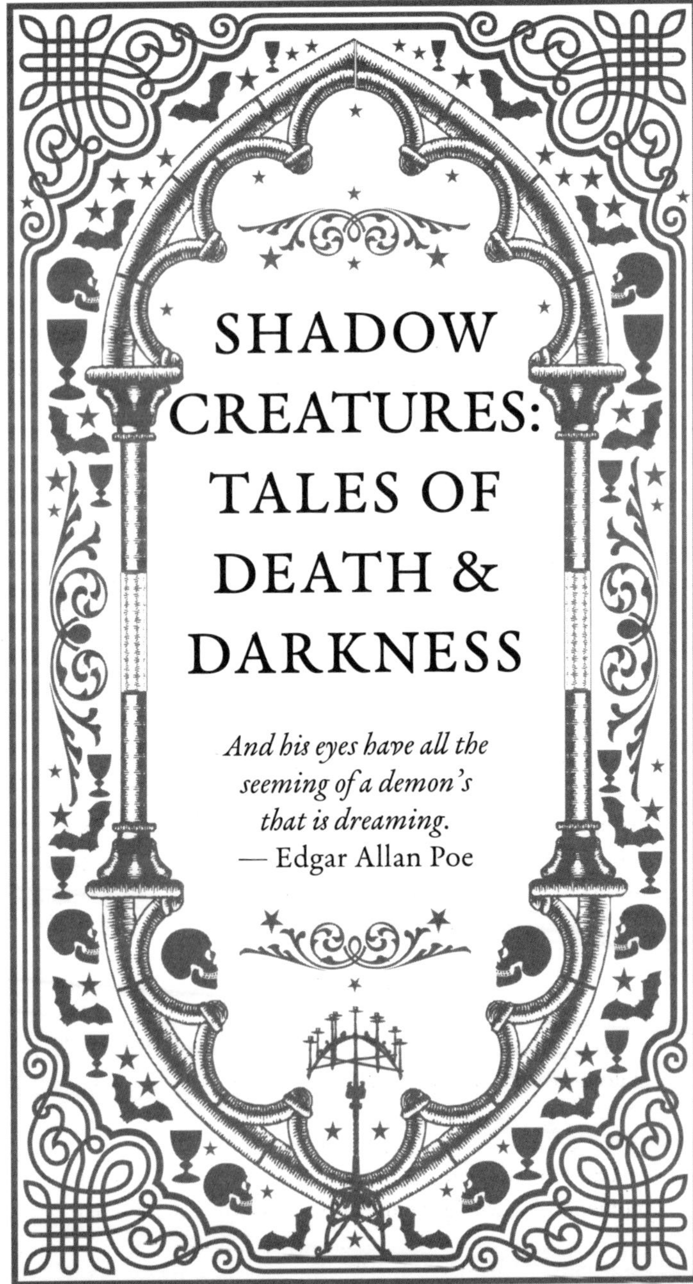
SHADOW
CREATURES:
TALES OF
DEATH &
DARKNESS
And his eyes have all the
seeming of a demon's
that is dreaming.
— Edgar Allan Poe

from THE WERE-WOLF

CLEMENCE HOUSMAN

She came.

She came with a smooth, gliding, noiseless speed, that was neither walking nor running; her arms were folded in her furs that were drawn tight about her body; the white lappets from her head were wrapped and knotted closely beneath her face; her eyes were set on a far distance. So she went till the even sway of her going was startled to a pause by Christian.

"Fell!"

She drew a quick, sharp breath at the sound of her name thus mutilated, and faced Sweyn's brother. Her eyes glittered; her upper lip was lifted, and shewed the teeth. The half of her name, impressed with an ominous sense as uttered by him, warned her of the aspect of a deadly foe. Yet she cast loose her robes till they trailed ample, and spoke as a mild woman.

"What would you?"

Then Christian answered with his solemn dreadful accusation:

"You kissed Rol — and Rol is dead! You kissed Trella: she is dead! You have kissed Sweyn, my brother; but he shall not die!"

He added: "You may live till midnight."

The edge of the teeth and the glitter of the eyes stayed a moment, and her right hand also slid down to the axe haft.

Then, without a word, she swerved from him, and sprang out and away swiftly over the snow.

And Christian sprang out and away, and followed her swiftly over the snow, keeping behind, but half-a-stride's length from her side.

So they went running together, silent, towards the vast wastes of snow, where no living thing but they two moved under the stars of night.

Never before had Christian so rejoiced in his powers. The gift of speed, and the training of use and endurance were priceless to him now. Though midnight was hours away, he was confident that, go where that Fell Thing would, hasten as she would, she could not outstrip him nor escape from him. Then, when came the time for transformation, when the woman's form made no longer a shield against a man's hand, he could slay or be slain to save Sweyn. He had struck his dear brother in dire extremity, but he could not, though reason urged, strike a woman.

For one mile, for two miles they ran: White Fell ever foremost, Christian ever at equal distance from her side, so near that, now and again, her out-flying furs touched him. She spoke no word; nor he. She never turned her head to look at him, nor swerved to evade him; but, with set face looking forward, sped straight on, over rough, over smooth, aware of his nearness by the regular beat of his feet, and the sound of his breath behind.

In a while she quickened her pace. From the first, Christian had judged of her speed as admirable, yet with exulting security in his own excelling and enduring whatever her efforts. But, when the pace increased, he found himself put to the test as never had he been before in any race. Her feet, indeed, flew faster than his; it was only by his length of stride that he kept his place at her side. But his heart was high and resolute, and he did not fear failure yet.

So the desperate race flew on. Their feet struck up the powdery snow, their breath smoked into the sharp clear air, and they were gone before the air was cleared of snow and vapour. Now and then Christian glanced up to judge, by the rising of the stars, of the coming of midnight. So long — so long!

White Fell held on without slack. She, it was evident, with confidence in her speed proving matchless, as resolute to outrun her pursuer as he to endure till midnight and fulfil his purpose. And Christian held on, still self-assured. He could not fail; he would not fail. To avenge Rol and Trella was motive enough for him to do what man could do; but for Sweyn more. She had kissed Sweyn, but he should not die too: with Sweyn to save he could not fail.

Never before was such a race as this; no, not when in old Greece man and maid raced together with two fates at stake; for the hard running was sustained unabated, while star after star rose and went wheeling up towards midnight, for one hour, for two hours.

Then Christian saw and heard what shot him through with fear. Where a fringe of trees hung round a slope he saw something dark moving, and heard a yelp, followed by a full horrid cry, and the dark spread out upon the snow, a pack of wolves in pursuit.

Of the beasts alone he had little cause for fear; at the pace he held he could distance them, four-footed though they were. But of White Fell's wiles he had infinite apprehension, for how might she not avail herself of the savage jaws of these wolves, akin as they were to half her nature. She vouchsafed to them nor look nor sign; but Christian, on an impulse to assure himself that she should not escape him, caught and held the back-flung edge of her furs, running still.

She turned like a flash with a beastly snarl, teeth and eyes gleaming again. Her axe shone, on the upstroke, on the downstroke, as she hacked at his hand. She had lopped it off at the wrist, but that he parried with the bear-spear. Even then, she shore through the shaft and shattered the bones of the hand at the same blow, so that he loosed perforce.

Then again they raced on as before, Christian not losing a pace, though his left hand swung useless, bleeding and broken.

The snarl, indubitable, though modified from a woman's organs, the vicious fury revealed in teeth and eyes, the sharp arrogant pain of her maiming blow, caught away Christian's heed of the beasts behind, by striking into him close vivid realisation of the infinitely greater danger that ran before him in that deadly Thing.

When he bethought him to look behind, lo! the pack had but reached their tracks, and instantly slunk aside, cowed; the yell of pursuit changing to yelps and whines. So abhorrent was that fell creature to beast as to man.

She had drawn her furs more closely to her, disposing them so that, instead of flying loose to her heels, no drapery hung lower than her knees, and this without a check to her wonderful speed, nor embarrassment by the cumbering of the folds. She held her head as before; her lips were firmly set, only the tense nostrils gave her breath; not a sign of distress witnessed to the long sustaining of that terrible speed.

But on Christian by now the strain was telling palpably. His head weighed heavy, and his breath came labouring in great sobs; the bear spear would have been a burden now. His heart was beating like a hammer, but such a dulness oppressed his brain, that it was only by degrees he could realise his helpless state; wounded and weaponless, chasing that terrible Thing, that was a fierce, desperate, axe-armed woman, except she should assume the beast with fangs yet more formidable.

And still the far slow stars went lingering nearly an hour from midnight.

So far was his brain astray that an impression took him that she was fleeing from the midnight stars, whose gain was by such slow degrees that a time equalling days and days had gone in the race round the northern circle of the world, and days and days as long might last before the end — except she slackened, or except he failed.

But he would not fail yet.

How long had he been praying so? He had started with a self-confidence and reliance that had felt no need for that aid; and now it seemed the only means by which to restrain his heart from swelling beyond the compass of his body, by which to cherish his brain from dwindling and shrivelling quite away. Some sharp-toothed creature kept tearing and dragging on his maimed left hand; he never could see it, he could not shake it off; but he prayed it off at times.

The clear stars before him took to shuddering, and he knew why: they shuddered at sight of what was behind him. He had never divined before that strange things hid themselves from men under pretence of being snow-clad mounds or swaying trees; but now they came slipping out from their harmless covers to follow him, and mock at his impotence to make a kindred Thing resolve to truer form. He knew the air behind him was thronged; he heard the hum of innumerable murmurings together; but his eyes could never catch them, they were too swift and nimble. Yet he knew they were there, because, on a backward glance, he saw the snow mounds surge as they grovelled flatlings out of sight; he saw the trees reel as they screwed themselves rigid past recognition among the boughs.

And after such glance the stars for awhile returned to steadfastness, and an infinite stretch of silence froze upon the chill grey world, only deranged by the swift even beat of the flying feet, and his own – slower from the longer stride, and the sound of his breath. And for some clear moments he knew that his only concern was, to sustain his speed regardless of pain and distress, to deny with every nerve he had her power to outstrip him or to widen the space between them, till the stars crept up to midnight. Then out again would come that crowd invisible, humming and hustling behind, dense and dark enough, he knew, to blot out the stars at his back, yet ever skipping and jerking from his sight.

A hideous check came to the race. White Fell swirled about and leapt to the right, and Christian, unprepared for so prompt a lurch, found close at his feet a deep pit yawning, and his own impetus past control. But he snatched at her as he bore past, clasping her right arm with his one whole hand, and the two swung together upon the brink.

And her straining away in self preservation was vigorous enough to counter-balance his headlong impulse, and brought them reeling together to safety.

Then, before he was verily sure that they were not to perish so, crashing down, he saw her gnashing in wild pale fury as she wrenched to be free; and since her right hand was in his grasp, used her axe left-handed, striking back at him.

The blow was effectual enough even so; his right arm dropped powerless, gashed, and with the lesser bone broken, that jarred with horrid pain when he let it swing as he leaped out again, and ran to recover the few feet she had gained from his pause at the shock.

The near escape and this new quick pain made again every faculty alive and intense. He knew that what he followed was most surely Death animate: wounded and helpless, he was utterly at her mercy if so she should realise and take action. Hopeless to avenge, hopeless to save, his very despair for Sweyn swept him on to follow, and follow, and precede the kiss-doomed to death. Could he yet fail to hunt that Thing past midnight, out of the womanly form alluring and treacherous, into lasting restraint of the bestial, which was the last shred of hope left from the confident purpose of the outset?

DARKNESS AND THE SHADOW

EDMUND CLARENCE STEDMAN

Waking, I have been nigh to Death, —
Have felt the chillness of his breath
Whiten my cheek and numb my heart,
And wondered why he stayed his dart, —
Yet quailed not, but could meet him so,
As any lesser friend or foe.
But sleeping, in the dreams of night,
His phantom stifles me with fright!
O God! what frozen horrors fall
Upon me with his visioned pall:
The movelessness, the unknown dread,
Fair life to pulseless silence wed!
And is the grave so darkly deep,
So hopeless, as it seems in sleep?
Can our sweet selves the coffin hold
So dumb within its crumbling mould?
And is the shroud so dank and drear
A garb, — the noisome worm so near?
Where then is Heaven's mercy fled, —
To quite forget the voiceless dead?

SHADOW OF NIGHTMARE

CLARK ASHTON SMITH

What hand is this, that unresisted grips
My spirit as with chains, and from the sound
And light of dreams, compels me to the bound
Where darkness waits with wide, expectant lips?
Albeit thereat my footing holds, nor slips,
The threats of that Omnipotence confound
All days and hours of gladness, girt around
With sense of near, unswervable eclipse.

So lies a land whose noon is plagued with whirr
Of bats, than their own shadows swarthier,
Whose flight is traced on roofs of white abodes,
Wherein from court to court, from room to room,
In hieroglyphics of abhorrent doom,
Is slowly trailed the slime of crawling toads.

from
THE PHANTOM HAG

W BOB HOLLAND

The other evening in an old castle the conversation turned upon apparitions, each one of the party telling a story. As the accounts grew more horrible the young ladies drew closer together.

"Have you ever had an adventure with a ghost?" said they to me. "Do you not know a story to make us shiver? Come, tell us something."

"I am quite willing to do so," I replied. "I will tell you of an incident that happened to myself."

Toward the close of the autumn of 1858 I visited one of my friends, sub-prefect of a little city in the center of France. Albert was an old companion of my youth, and I had been present at his wedding. His charming wife was full of goodness and grace. My friend wished to show me his happy home, and to introduce me to his two pretty little daughters. I was feted and taken great care of. Three days after my arrival I knew the entire city, curiosities, old castles, ruins, etc. Every day about four o'clock Albert would order the phaeton, and we would take a long ride, returning home in the evening. One evening my friend said to me:

"To-morrow we will go further than usual. I want to take you to the Black Rocks. They are curious old Druidical stones, on a wild and desolate plain. They will interest you. My wife has not seen them yet, so we will take her."

The following day we drove out at the usual hour. Albert's wife sat by his side. I occupied the back seat alone. The weather was gray and somber that afternoon, and the journey was not very pleasant. When we arrived at the Black Rocks the sun was setting. We got out of the phaeton, and Albert took care of the horses.

We walked some little distance through the fields before reaching the giant remains of the old Druid religion. Albert's wife wished to climb to the summit of the altar, and I assisted her. I can still see her graceful figure as she stood draped in a red shawl, her veil floating around her.

"How beautiful it is! But does it not make you feel a little melancholy?" said she, extending her hand toward the dark horizon, which was lighted a little by the last rays of the sun.

The afternoon wind blew violently, and sighed through the stunted trees that grew around the stone cromlechs; not a dwelling nor a human being was in sight. We hastened to get down, and silently retraced our steps to the carriage.

"We must hurry," said Albert; "the sky is threatening, and we shall have scarcely time to reach home before night."

We carefully wrapped the robes around his wife. She tied the veil around her face, and the horses started into a rapid trot. It was growing dark; the scenery around us was bare and desolate; clumps of fir trees here and there and furze bushes formed the only vegetation. We began to feel the cold, for the wind blew with fury; the only sound we heard was the steady trot of the horses and the sharp clear tinkle of their bells.

Suddenly I felt the heavy grasp of a hand upon my shoulder. I turned my head quickly. A horrible apparition presented itself before my eyes. In the empty place at my side sat a hideous woman. I tried to cry out; the phantom placed her fingers upon her lips to impose silence upon me. I could not utter a sound. The woman was clothed in white linen; her head was cowled; her face was overspread with a corpse-like pallor, and in place of eyes were ghastly black cavities.

I sat motionless, overcome by terror.

The ghost suddenly stood up and leaned over the young wife. She encircled her with her arms, and lowered her hideous head as if to kiss her forehead.

"What a wind!" cried Madame Albert, turning precipitately toward me. "My veil is torn."

As she turned I felt the same infernal pressure on my shoulder, and the place occupied by the phantom was empty.

I looked out to the right and left — the road was deserted, not an object in sight.

"What a dreadful gale!" said Madame Albert. "Did you feel it? I cannot explain the terror that seized me; my veil was torn by the wind as if by an invisible hand; I am trembling still."

"Never mind," said Albert, smiling; "wrap yourself up, my dear; we will soon be warming ourselves by a good fire at home. I am starving."

A cold perspiration covered my forehead; a shiver ran through me; my tongue clove to the roof of my mouth, and I could not articulate a sound; a sharp pain in my shoulder was the only sensible evidence that I was not the victim of an hallucination. Putting my hand upon my aching shoulder, I felt a rent in the cloak that was wrapped around me. I looked at it; five perfectly distinct holes — visible traces of the grip of the horrible phantom. I thought for a moment that I should die or that my reason should leave me; it was, I think, the most dreadful moment of my life.

Finally I became more calm; this nameless agony had lasted for some minutes; I do not think it is possible for a human being to suffer more than I did during that time. As soon as I had recovered my senses, I thought at first I would tell my friends all that had passed, but hesitated, and finally did not, fearing that my story would frighten Madame Albert, and feeling sure my friend would not believe me. The lights of the little city revived me, and gradually the oppression of terror that overwhelmed me became lighter.

So soon as we reached home, Madame Albert untied her veil; it was literally in shreds. I hoped to find my clothes whole and prove to myself that it was all imagination. But no, the cloth was torn in five places, just where the fingers had seized my shoulder. There was no mark, however, upon my flesh, only a dull pain.

I returned to Paris the next day, where I endeavored to forget the strange adventure; or at least when I thought of it, I would force myself to think it an hallucination.

THE BANSHEE

DORA SIGERSON SHORTER

Now God between us and all harm,
For I to-night have seen
A banshee in the shadow pass
Along the dark boreen.
And as she went she keened and cried
And combed her long white hair,
She stopped at Molly Reilly's door,
And sobbed till midnight there.
And is it for himself she moans,
Who is so far away?
Or is it Molly Reilly's death
She cries until the day?
Now Molly thinks her man is gone
A sailor lad to be;
She puts a candle at her door
Each night for him to see.
But he is off to Galway town,
(And who dare tell her this?)
Enchanted by a woman's eyes,
Half-maddened by her kiss.
So as we go by Molly's door
We look towards the sea,
And say, "May God bring home your lad,
Wherever he may be."
I pray it may be Molly's self
The banshee keens and cries,
For who dare breathe the tale to her,
Be it her man who dies?
But there is sorrow on the way,
For I to-night have seen
A banshee in the shadow pass
Along the dark boreen.

from
MACBETH

WILLIAM SHAKESPEARE

Three witches, casting a spell ...

Round about the cauldron go;
In the poison'd entrails throw.
Toad, that under cold stone
Days and nights hast thirty one
Swelter'd venom sleeping got,
Boil thou first i' the charmed pot.

Double, double toil and trouble;
Fire burn and cauldron bubble.

Fillet of a fenny snake,
In the cauldron boil and bake;
Eye of newt, and toe of frog,
Wool of bat, and tongue of dog,
Adder's fork, and blind-worm's sting,
Lizard's leg, and howlet's wing,
For a charm of powerful trouble,
Like a hell-broth boil and bubble.

Double, double toil and trouble;
Fire burn and cauldron bubble.

from THE WITCHES' SABBATH

CONRAD AIKEN

Now, when the moon slid under the cloud
And the cold clear dark of starlight fell,
He heard in his blood the well-known bell
Tolling slowly in heaves of sound,
Slowly beating, slowly beating,
Shaking its pulse on the stagnant air:
Sometimes it swung completely round,
Horribly gasping as if for breath;
Falling down with an anguished cry…
Now the red bat, he mused, will fly;
Something is marked, this night, for death…
And while he mused, along his blood
Flew ghostly voices, remote and thin,
They rose in the cavern of his brain,
Like ghosts they died away again;
And hands upon his heart were laid,
And music upon his flesh was played,
Until, as he was bidden to do,
He walked the wood he so well knew.
Through the cold dew he moved his feet,
And heard far off, as under the earth,
Discordant music in shuddering tones,
Screams of laughter, horrible mirth,
Clapping of hands, and thudding of drums,
And the long-drawn wail of one in pain.
To-night, he thought, I shall die again,
We shall die again in the red-eyed fire
To meet on the edge of the wood beyond

With the placid gaze of fed desire...
He walked; and behind the whisper of trees,
In and out, one walked with him:
She parted the branches and peered at him,
Through lowered lids her two eyes burned,
He heard her breath, he saw her hand,
Wherever he turned his way, she turned:
Kept pace with him, now fast, now slow;
Moving her white knees as he moved...
This is the one I have always loved;
This is the one whose bat-soul comes
To dance with me, flesh to flesh,
In the starlight dance of horns and drums...

The walls and roofs, the scarlet towers,
Sank down behind a rushing sky.
He heard a sweet song just begun
Abruptly shatter in tones and die.
It whirled away. Cold silence fell.
And again came tollings of a bell.

This air is alive with witches: the white witch rides
Swifter than smoke on the starlit wind.
In the clear darkness, while the moon hides,
They come like dreams, like something remembered...
Let us hurry! beloved; take my hand,
Forget these things that trouble your eyes,
Forget, forget! Our flesh is changed,
Lighter than smoke we wreathe and rise...

INCANTATION

GEORGE PARSONS LATHROP

When the leaves, by thousands thinned,
A thousand times have whirled in the wind,
And the moon, with hollow cheek,
Staring from her hollow height,
Consolation seems to seek
From the dim, reechoing night;
And the fog-streaks dead and white
Lie like ghosts of lost delight
O'er highest earth and lowest sky;
Then, Autumn, work thy witchery!

Strew the ground with poppy-seeds,
And let my bed be hung with weeds,
Growing gaunt and rank and tall,
Drooping o'er me like a pall.
Send thy stealthy, white-eyed mist
Across my brow to turn and twist
Fold on fold, and leave me blind
To all save visions in the mind.
Then, in the depth of rain-fed streams
I shall slumber, and in dreams
Slide through some long glen that burns
With a crust of blood-red ferns
And brown-withered wings of brake
Like a burning lava-lake; —
So, urged to fearful, faster flow
By the awful gasp, "Hahk! hahk!" of the crow,
Shall pass by many a haunted rood

Of the nutty, odorous wood;
Or, where the hemlocks lean and loom,
Shall fill my heart with bitter gloom;
Till, lured by light, reflected cloud,
I burst aloft my watery shroud,
And upward through the ether sail
Far above the shrill wind's wail; —
But, falling thence, my soul involve
With the dust dead flowers dissolve;
And, gliding out at last to sea,
Lulled to a long tranquillity,
The perfect poise of seasons keep
With the tides that rest at neap.
So must be fulfilled the rite
That giveth me the dead year's might;
And at dawn I shall arise
A spirit, though with human eyes,
A human form and human face;
And where'er I go or stay,
There the summer's perished grace
Shall be with me, night and day.

THE WERE-WOLF

MADISON JULIUS CAWEIN

SHE.
Nay; still amort, my love? Why dost thou lag?
HE.
The strix-owl cried.
SHE.
Nay! yon wild stream that leaps
Hoarse from the black pines of the Hakel steeps,
A moon-tipped water, down a glittering crag.--
Why so aghast, sweetheart? Why dost thou stop?
HE.
The demon-huntsman passed with hooting horn!
SHE.
Nay! 't was the blind wind sweeping through the thorn
Around the ruins of the Dumburg's top.
HE.
My limbs are cold.
SHE.
Come! warm thee in mine arms.
HE.
Mine eyes are weary.
SHE.
Rest them, love, on mine.
HE.
I am athirst.
SHE.
Quench on my lips thy thirst. –
O dear belovéd, how thy last kiss warms
My blood again!
HE.
Off!... How thy eyeballs shine!
Thy face!... thy form!... So do I die accursed!

THE SICK MUSE

CHARLES BAUDELAIRE

Poor Muse, alas, what ails thee, then, to-day?
Thy hollow eyes with midnight visions burn,
Upon thy brow in alternation play,
Folly and Horror, cold and taciturn.

Have the green lemure and the goblin red,
Poured on thee love and terror from their urn?
Or with despotic hand the nightmare dread
Deep plunged thee in some fabulous Minturne?

Would that the breast where so deep thoughts arise,
Breathed forth a healthful perfume with thy sighs;
Would that thy Christian blood ran wave by wave

In rhythmic sounds the antique numbers gave,
When Phoebus shared his alternating reign
With mighty Pan, lord of the ripening grain.

THE LOVES OF THE PLANTS

ERASMUS DARWIN

So on his NIGHTMARE through the evening fog
Flits the squab Fiend o'er fen, and lake, and bog;
Seeks some love-wilder'd Maid with sleep oppress'd,
Alights, and grinning fits upon her breast.

Such as of late amid the murky sky
Was mark'd by Fuseli's poetic eye;
Whose daring tints, with Shakespear's happiest grace,
Gave to the airy phantom form and place. —
Back o'er her pillow sinks her blushing head,

Her snow-white limbs hang helpless from the bed;
While with quick sighs, and suffocative breath,
Her interrupted heart-pulse swims in death.
Then shrieks of captured towns, and widows' tears,
Pale lovers stretch'd upon their blood-stain'd biers,

The headlong precipice that thwarts her flight,
The trackless desert, the cold starless night,
And stern-eye'd Murder with his knife behind,
In dread succession agonize her mind.
O'er her fair limbs convulsive tremors fleet,
Start in her hands, and struggle in her feet;
In vain to scream with quivering lips she tries,
And strains in palsy'd lids her tremulous eyes;
In vain she wills to run, fly, swim, walk, creep;
The WILL presides not in the bower of SLEEP.

On her fair bosom sits the Demon-Ape
Erect, and balances his bloated shape;
Rolls in their marble orbs his Gorgon-eyes,
And drinks with leathern ears her tender cries.

THE DANCE OF DEATH (TOTENTANZ)

JOHANN WOLFGANG VON GOETHE

The warder looks down at the mid hour of night,
On the tombs that lie scatter'd below:
The moon fills the place with her silvery light,
And the churchyard like day seems to glow.
When see! first one grave, then another opes wide,
And women and men stepping forth are descried,
In cerements snow-white and trailing. –

In haste for the sport soon their ankles they twitch,
And whirl round in dances so gay;
The young and the old, and the poor, and the rich,
But the cerements stand in their way;
And as modesty cannot avail them aught here,
They shake themselves all, and the shrouds soon appear
Scatter'd over the tombs in confusion. –

Now waggles the leg, and now wriggles the thigh,
As the troop with strange gestures advance,
And a rattle and clatter anon rises high,
As of one beating time to the dance.
The sight to the warder seems wondrously queer,
When the villainous Tempter speaks thus in his ear:
"Seize one of the shrouds that lie yonder!" –

* * *

Quick as thought it was done! and for safety he fled
Behind the church-door with all speed;
The moon still continues her clear light to shed
On the dance that they fearfully lead.
But the dancers at length disappear one by one,
And their shrouds, ere they vanish, they carefully don,
And under the turf all is quiet.

But one of them stumbles and shuffles there still,
And gropes at the graves in despair;
Yet 'tis by no comrade he's treated so ill
The shroud he soon scents in the air.
So he rattles the door — for the warder 'tis well
That 'tis bless'd, and so able the foe to repel,
All cover'd with crosses in metal. —

The shroud he must have, and no rest will allow,
There remains for reflection no time;
On the ornaments Gothic the wight seizes now,
And from point on to point hastes to climb.
Alas for the warder! his doom is decreed!
Like a long-legged spider, with ne'er-changing speed,
Advances the dreaded pursuer. —

The warder he quakes, and the warder turns pale,
The shroud to restore fain had sought;
When the end, — now can nothing to save him avail, —
In a tooth formed of iron is caught.
With vanishing lustre the moon's race is run,
When the bell thunders loudly a powerful One,
And the skeleton fails, crush'd to atoms.

THE BANSHEE

DONALD A MACKENZIE

Knee-deep she waded in the pool –
The Banshee robed in green –
She sang yon song the whole night long,
And washed the linen clean;
The linen that would wrap the dead
She beetled on a stone,
She stood with dripping hands, blood-red,
Low singing all alone –
His linen robes are pure and white,
For Fergus More must die to-night!

'Twas Fergus More rode o'er the hill,
Come back from foreign wars,
His horse's feet were clattering sweet
Below the pitiless stars;
And in his heart he would repeat –
"O never again I'll roam;
All weary is the going forth,
But sweet the coming home!"
His linen robes are pure and white,
For Fergus More must die to-night!

He saw the blaze upon his hearth
Come gleaming down the glen;
For he was fain for home again,
And rode before his men –
"'Tis many a weary day," he'd sigh,
"Since I would leave her side;

* * *

I'll never more leave Scotland's shore
And yon, my dark-eyed bride."
His linen robes are pure and white,
For Fergus More must die to-night!

So dreaming of her tender love,
Soft tears his eyes would blind –
When up there crept and swiftly leapt
A man who stabbed behind –
"'Tis you," he cried, "who stole my bride,
This night shall be your last!"...
When Fergus fell, the warm, red tide
Of life came ebbing fast...
His linen robes are pure and white,
For Fergus More must die to-night!

THE DEMON OF THE GIBBET

FITZ-JAMES O'BRIEN

There was no west, there was no east,
No star abroad for eye to see;
And Norman spurred his jaded beast
Hard by the terrible gallows-tree.

"O Norman, haste across this waste —
For something seems to follow me!"
"Cheer up, dear Maud, for, thanked be God,
We nigh have passed the gallows-tree!"

He kissed her lip; then — spur and whip!
And fast they fled across the lea!
But vain the heel and rowel steel, —
For something leaped from the gallows-tree!

"Give me your cloak, your knightly cloak,
That wrapped you oft beyond the sea;
The wind is bold, my bones are old,
And I am cold on the gallows-tree."

"O holy God! O dearest Maud,
Quick, quick, some prayers, — the best that be!
A bony hand my neck has spanned,
And tears my knightly cloak from me!"

* * *

"Give me your wine, — the red, red wine,
That in the flask hangs by your knee!
Ten summers burst on me accurst,
And I'm athirst on the gallows-tree."

"O Maud, my life! my loving wife!
Have you no prayer to set us free?
My belt unclasps, — a demon grasps
And drags my wine-flask from my knee!"

"Give me your bride, your bonnie bride,
That left her nest with you to flee!
O, she hath flown to be my own,
For I'm alone on the gallows-tree!"

"Cling closer, Maud, and trust in God!
Cling close! — Ah, heaven, she slips from me!" —
A prayer, a groan, and he alone
Rode on that night from the gallows-tree.

from THE ONI ON HIS TRAVELS

WILLIAM ELLIOT GRIFFIS

Across the ocean, in Japan, there once lived curious creatures called Onis. Every Japanese boy and girl has heard of them, though one has not often been caught. In one museum, visitors could see the hairy leg of a specimen. Falling out of the air in a storm, the imp had lost his limb. It had been torn off by being caught in the timber side of a well curb. The story-teller was earnestly assured by one Japanese lad that his grandfather had seen it tumble from the clouds.

Many people are sure that the Onis live in the clouds and occasionally fall off, during a peal of thunder. Then they escape and hide down in a well. Or, they get loose in the kitchen, rattle the dishes around, and make a great racket. They behave like cats, with a dog after them. They do a great deal of mischief, but not much harm. There are even some old folks who say that, after all, Onis are only unruly children, that behave like angels in the morning and act like imps in the afternoon. So we see that not much is known about the Onis.

Many things that go wrong are blamed on the Onis. Foolish folks, such as stupid maid-servants, and dull-witted fellows, that blunder a good deal, declare that the Onis made them do it. Drunken men, especially, that stumble into mud-holes at night, say the Onis pushed them in. Naughty boys that steal cake, and girls that take sugar, often tell fibs to their parents, charging it on the Onis.

The Onis love to play jokes on people, but they are not dangerous. There are plenty of pictures of them in Japan, though they never sat for their portraits, but this is the way they looked.

Some Onis have only one eye in their forehead, others two, and, once in a while, a big fellow has three. There are little, short horns on their heads, but these are no bigger than those on a baby deer and never grow long. The hair on their heads gets all snarled up, just like a little girl's that cries when her tangled tresses are combed out; for the Onis make use of neither brushes nor looking glasses. As for their faces, they never wash them, so they look sooty. Their skin is rough, like an elephant's. On each of their feet are only three toes. Whether an Oni has a nose, or a snout, is not agreed upon by the learned men who have studied them.

No one ever heard of an Oni being higher than a yardstick, but they are so strong that one of them can easily lift two bushel bags of rice at once. In Japan, they steal the food offered to the idols. They can live without air. They like nothing better than to drink both the rice spirit called saké, and the black liquid called soy, of which only a few drops, as a sauce on fish, are enough for a man. Of this sauce, the Dutch, as well as the Japanese, are very fond.

Above all things else, the most fun for a young Oni is to get into a crockery shop. Once there, he jumps round among the cups and dishes, hides in the jars, straddles the shelves and turns somersaults over the counter. In fact, the Oni is only a jolly little imp. The Japanese girls, on New Year's eve, throw handfuls of dried beans in every room of the house and cry, "In, with good luck; and out with you, Onis!" Yet they laugh merrily all the time. The Onis cannot speak, but they can chatter like monkeys. They often seem to be talking to each other in gibberish.

Now it once happened in Japan that the great Tycoon of the country wanted to make a present to the Prince of the Dutch. So he sent all over the land, from the sweet potato fields in the south to the seal and salmon waters in the north, to get curiosities of all sorts. The products of Japan, from the warm parts, where grow the indigo and the sugar cane, to the cold regions, in which are the bear and walrus, were sent as gifts to go to the Land of Dykes and Windmills. The Japanese had heard that the Dutch people like cheese, walk in wooden shoes, eat with forks, instead of chopsticks, and the women wear twenty petticoats apiece, while the men sport jackets with two gold buttons, and folks generally do things the other way from that which was common in Japan.

Now it chanced that while they were packing the things that were piled up in the palace at Yedo, a young Oni, with his horns only half grown, crawled into the kitchen, at night, through the big bamboo water pipe near the pump. Pretty soon he jumped into the storeroom. There, the precious cups, vases, lacquer boxes, pearl-inlaid pill-holders, writing desks, jars of tea, and bales of silk, were lying about, ready to be put into their cases. The yellow wrappings for covering the pretty things of gold and silver, bronze and wood, and the rice chaff, for the packing of the porcelain, were all at hand. What a jolly time the Oni did have, in tumbling them about and rolling over them! Then he leaped like a monkey from one vase to another. He put on a lady's gay silk kimono and wrapped himself around with golden embroidery. Then he danced and played the game of the Ka-gu'-ra, or Lion of Korea, pretending to make love to a girl-Oni. Such funny capers as he did cut! It would have made a cat laugh to see him. It was broad daylight, before his pranks were over, and the Dutch church chimes were playing the hour of seven.

Suddenly the sound of keys in the lock told him that, in less than a minute, the door would open.

Where should he hide? There was no time to be lost. So he seized some bottles of soy from the kitchen shelf and then jumped into the big bottom drawer of a ladies' cabinet, and pulled it shut.

"Namu Amida" (Holy Buddha!), cried the man that opened the door. "Who has been here? It looks like a rat's picnic." However, the workmen soon came and set everything to rights. Then they packed up the pretty things. They hammered down the box lids and before night the Japanese curiosities were all stored in the hold of a swift, Dutch ship, from Nagasaki, bound for Rotterdam. After a long voyage, the vessel arrived safely in good season, and the boxes were sent on to The Hague, or capital city. As the presents were for the Prince, they were taken at once to the pretty palace, called the House in the Wood. There they were unpacked and set on exhibition for the Prince and Princess to see the next day.

When the palace maid came in next morning to clean up the floor and dust the various articles, her curiosity led her to pull open the drawer of the ladies' cabinet; when out jumped something hairy. It nearly frightened the girl out of her wits. It was the Oni, which rushed off and down stairs, tumbling over a half dozen servants, who were sitting at their breakfast. All started to run except the brave butler, who caught up a carving knife and showed fight. Seeing this, the Oni ran down into the cellar, hoping to find some hole or crevice for escape. All around, were shelves filled with cheeses, jars of sour-krout, pickled herring, and stacks of fresh rye bread standing in the corners. But oh! how they did smell in his Japanese nostrils! Oni, as he was, he nearly fainted, for no such odors had ever beaten upon his nose, when in Japan. Even at the risk of being carved into bits, he must go back. So up into the kitchen again he ran. Happily, the door into the garden stood wide open.

Grabbing a fresh bottle of soy from the kitchen shelf, the Oni, with a hop, skip and jump, reached outdoors. Seeing a pair of klomps, or wooden shoes, near the steps, the Oni put his pair of three toes into them, to keep the dogs from scenting its tracks. Then he ran into the fields, hiding among the cows, until he heard men with pitchforks coming. At once the Oni leaped upon a cow's back and held on to its horns, while the poor animal ran for its life into its stall, in the cow stable, hoping to brush the monster off.

from THE DEVILS AND EVIL SPIRITS OF BABYLONIA

R CAMPBELL THOMPSON

Spirits that minish heaven and earth,
That minish the land,
Spirits that minish the land,
Of giant strength,
Of giant strength and giant tread,
Demons (like) raging bulls, great ghosts,
Ghosts that break through all houses,
Demons that have no shame,
Seven are they!
Knowing no care,
They grind the land like corn;
Knowing no mercy,
They rage against mankind:
They spill their blood like rain,
Devouring their flesh (and) sucking their veins.
Where the images of the gods are, there they quake
In the temple of Nabu, who fertiliseth the shoots of wheat.
They are demons full of violence
Ceaselessly devouring blood.
Invoke the ban against them,
That they no more return to this neighbourhood.
By Heaven be ye exorcised! By Earth be ye exorcised!

WERE-WOLF

JULIAN HAWTHORNE

RUNS the wind along the waste,
Run the clouds across the moon,
Ghastly shadows run in haste
From snowy dune to dune —
Blue shadows o'er the ghastly white
Spectral gleaming in the night.
But ghastlier, more spectral still,
What fearful thing speeds hither,
Running, running, running
Swifter than cloud or wind?
What omen of nameless ill,
Whence coming, speeding whither,
Running, running, running,
Leaves all save fear behind?
Leaning, leaning in the race,
Breath keen-drawn through nostrils tense,
Fell eyes in ruthless face,
What goblin of malevolence
Runs through the frozen night
In superhuman flight?
See it run, run, run,
Outstripping the shadows that fly!
Hear the fiend's heart beat, beat,
Beat, beat, beat in its breast!
Running, running, running on
Under the frozen sky,
Fleet, so fearfully fleet,
Pausing never to rest.
Clutched — what is clutched so tight

In its lean, cold hands as it speeds?
Something soft, something white,
Something human, that bleeds?
Is it an infant's curly head,
And innocent limbs, gnawed and red?
Fleeter and yet more fleet
It leans, leans and runs;
Dabbled with blood are its awful lips,
Grinning in horrible glee.
The wolves that follow with scurrying feet,
Sniffing that goblin scent, at once
Scatter in terror, while it slips
Away, to the shore of the frozen sea.
Away! is it man? is it woman,
On such dread meat to feed?
Away! is it beast? is it human?
Or is it a fiend indeed?
Fiend from human loins begotten,
Hell-inspired, God-forgotten!
Now the midnight hour draws on:
Human form no fiend may keep
Or ever that mystic hour is told.
Lower, lower, lower it bends.
Midnight is come — is come and gone!
Down on all fours see it plunge and leap!
A human yell in a wolf's howl ends!...
What gaunt, gray thing gallops on o'er the world?

THE HAG

ROBERT HERRICK

The Hag is astride
This night for to ride,
The Devill and shee together;
Through thick and through thin,
Now out and then in,
Though ne'er so foul be the weather.

A Thorn or a Burr
She takes for a Spurre,
With a lash of a Bramble she rides now;
Through Brakes and through Briars,
O'er Ditches and Mires,
She follows the Spirit that guides now.

No Beast for his food
Dares now range the wood,
But hush'd in his laire he lies lurking;
While mischiefs, by these,
On Land and on Seas,
At noone of Night are a-working.

The storme will arise
And trouble the skies;
This night, and more for the wonder,
The ghost from the Tomb
Affrighted shall come,
Call'd out by the clap of the Thunder.

HELENA

HEINRICH HEINE

Thou hast call'd me forth from out of the grave
By means of thy magic will now,
And fill'd me full of love's fierce glow –
This glow thou never canst still now.
O press thy mouth against my mouth,
Man's breath with heaven is scented;
Thy very soul I'll drain to the dregs,
The dead are never contented.

GHASTA, OR THE AVENGING DEMON

PERCY BYSSHE SHELLEY

Hark! the owlet flaps her wing,
In the pathless dell beneath,
Hark! night ravens loudly sing,
Tidings of despair and death. –

Horror covers all the sky,
Clouds of darkness blot the moon,
Prepare! for mortal thou must die,
Prepare to yield thy soul up soon –

Fierce the tempest raves around,
Fierce the volleyed lightnings fly,
Crashing thunder shakes the ground,
Fire and tumult fill the sky. –

Hark! the tolling village bell,
Tells the hour of midnight come,
Now can blast the powers of Hell,
Fiend-like goblins now can roam –

See! his crest all stained with rain,
A warrior hastening speeds his way,
He starts, looks round him, starts again,
And sighs for the approach of day.

See! his frantic steed he reins,
See! he lifts his hands on high,
Implores a respite to his pains,
From the powers of the sky. –

He seeks an Inn, for faint from toil,
Fatigue had bent his lofty form,
To rest his wearied limbs awhile,
Fatigued with wandering and the storm.

Slow the door is opened wide –
With trackless tread a stranger came,
His form Majestic, slow his stride,
He sate, nor spake, – nor told his name –

Terror blanched the warrior's cheek,
Cold sweat from his forehead ran,
In vain his tongue essayed to speak, –
At last the stranger thus began:

'Mortal! thou that saw'st the sprite,
Tell me what I wish to know,
Or come with me before 'tis light,
Where cypress trees and mandrakes grow.

'Fierce the avenging Demon's ire,
Fiercer than the wintry blast,
Fiercer than the lightning's fire,
When the hour of twilight's past' –

The warrior raised his sunken eye.
It met the stranger's sullen scowl,
'Mortal! Mortal! thou must die,'
In burning letters chilled his soul.